LINEAGE OF THE TREES

FIVE GENERATIONS

grandpa   grandma
abe   sarah

grandpa   grandma   aunt
breton   emmie   marie
(pa)   (ma)   (ma's sister)

uncle   aunt   belle
jesse   charlotte (lata's mom)

lata

[calla & millie]

OUR GREATEST RESPONSIBILITY
IS TO BE GOOD ANCESTORS.

JONAS SALK

LINEAGE
OF THE
TREES

a soul story

jane brunette

flaming seed
press

ISBN 978-0-9892605-5-8

Book design:
Jane Brunette

Published by:
Flamingseed Press, California

flamingseed.com

Contents

Part TWO

for my mother

my Grandma Ethyl Marie Brunette Brewer

Uncle Doc & Aunt Mary Brunette

the Menominee tribe

and all people struggling

to remember their place

in the lineage of the trees

Author's note

THIS BOOK is what I call a soul story. It is true in the way that myths and dreams are true and is best read through that lens. While it draws from the real history of the Menominee tribe and my own family history, it is a work of fiction.

The situations and characters emerged from my life experiences and concerns, but none of them represent factual events or individuals, living or dead. Rather, it is a mashup between history, people I have known, challenges I've encountered, and aspects of my soul.

Any historical implications that might unwittingly be misleading are due to my own ignorance and limitations as a writer.

—*Jane Brunette*

Part **ONE**

I NEVER SAW A TREE
THAT WAS NO TREE IN PARTICULAR.
—ANNIE DILLARD

1

THE WOMAN WHO SET FIRE TO HER LIFE

Lata

THE DAY BEFORE MY EIGHTH BIRTHDAY, my Aunt Charlotte poured gasoline in a crooked line through the house and put a match at one end. I stood on the front lawn where she told me to wait. The last time I saw her, she stood in the attic window waving at me, a solid wall of fire behind her like a stage curtain.

Even now, I can see her in the attic pouring the gasoline into boxes of old clothes, then dropping a match into each box. How brilliant that first moment must have been, the sudden burst of light and heat, and then flames dancing like spirits. She had a plan on how to get out through the back door, how she would drop me at Grandma Emmie's and go on by herself. She wouldn't say where, but wherever she went, I knew there would be trees — lots of them.

One can of gasoline would reduce the whole house to ash is what Aunt Charlotte told me, and it would happen while we were safe in the taxi, but she hadn't counted on Mrs. Petty deciding to remove the wilted geraniums from her front porch so early in the morning. When she saw the smoke, Mrs. Petty rushed back inside to call for help while I stood still on the lawn, watching the first tongue of fire emerge from the attic window and lick the roof. Silent witness to a fierce deity, I was — the breath of Kali with Aunt Charlotte as her carrier. Something in my girl-self knew this the way the belly knows things, but of course, I didn't have words to explain.

Still, it would take a lifetime to understand why Aunt Charlotte burned the house, and with it, the dreams of my sweet Uncle Jesse, who I last saw more than 40 years ago right there on the lawn, fire still thrashing from the windows. When he got the call, he raced home in his van, stopped with a violent jerk against the curb and left the door open, radio blasting, as he bolted toward the front porch with a force that required a firefighter and a police officer to restrain. They spoke firmly to him until his breath slowed and then he circled the lawn like a tiger as the hoses flooded his beloved house, his wife likely somewhere inside.

His eyes fell on me and instinctively he came, knelt before me on the lawn and put a hand on each of my shoulders. He was young then, and ruggedly handsome, dark hair falling like a question mark on his forehead, face bronzed and chiseled from a summer of hammering rooftops on tract houses. The eyes that looked out from him I barely recognized, so full of a wild and bewildered grief. He held my shoulders tight, urgent: *What did she say to you? What do you know?* But a strange silence had come over me and I was unable to move my lips — unable to move at all. I just stood there and looked into his eyes until I was lost in the deep blue lakes of them, floating on the water behind all the turbulence.

I understood why he didn't want to see me again. I saw

it then in his eyes: how they darkened into recognition and then fear as he shook my shoulders on the lawn and I was not there to answer. One of the firefighters led him away and a detective took me across the street to the screened porch of Mrs. Petty's house, where I sat on an old wicker couch with musty, daisy-print cushions and remained in that strange repose under the elder woman's nervous watch. She hovered, birdlike and flustered, serving me milk and packaged coffee cake until my mother collected me and brought me home.

Later, I overheard my mother tell Grandma Emmie not to be too hard on her son-in-law for avoiding me. "Jesse's crazy with grief," I heard her say. "And when he looks at Lata, he sees Charlotte's eyes." After that, when I looked in the mirror, I saw the eyes of the woman who had set fire to her life, and wondered where my own eyes had gone. Seeing through Aunt Charlotte's eyes, the world looked different: more harsh, more tender, and more strange.

Uncle Jesse told everyone that Aunt Charlotte died in the fire, but when I asked if I could see her body, my mother told me there wasn't anything to see. At first, I thought she might have been lying. She might not have wanted me to see her, blackened and shrunken, hollow sockets where her dark eyes had been. But I could never picture Aunt Charlotte that way — I could only picture the smoke gathering her up, freeing her from the house, and she, giddy with her sudden lightness, gliding off like a bird.

I later learned that when my mother said there was nothing to see, there really was nothing to see. Investigators searched the rubble for Aunt Charlotte's remains, but didn't have any luck. There was too much destruction. The roof had collapsed through the second floor, taking most of the interior walls with it, so the only things left standing were a small section of the front porch, the fieldstone fireplace along with part of its chimney, and the sunroom, which shared a stone wall with the fireplace. The rubble was heavy and deep. A charred black mess was what they were going through, and it didn't seem there was much hope of anything being found.

As it turned out, the varnish Uncle Jesse had used to re-finish the floors was highly flammable and toxic fumes still lingered, creating lung problems for the investigators, so who could blame them when their efforts petered out? Everyone was already certain that Aunt Charlotte was dead. What else could have happened to her? Mrs. Petty claimed to have seen her in the attic window, same as me. Everyone agreed that there was no chance anything could have come of Charlotte except to have turned to ash, now buried deep in that heap of rubble, indistinguishable from the charred remains of Uncle Jesse's house.

When investigators questioned me about Aunt Charlotte's motives, I told them the same thing she had told me: that she had burned the house in order to release Uncle Jesse from the prison he had built for himself so he could do what he was really meant to do. "She didn't think of it her-self," I told them and anyone else who asked. "The dreams told her to do it." I was certain this would absolve her in their eyes, but of course, no one understood. They tried to get me to change my story, but I kept insisting until they stopped asking. Still, everyone whispered about it and

I didn't like what they were saying—that what Aunt Charlotte had done was crazy, terrible and strange. Sometimes I had to fight those voices from seeping into me or they would have collapsed all the beauty and gift of her into their verdict of craziness, even as my belly told me that Aunt Charlotte was the sanest of them all.

Anyone could see that Aunt Charlotte was different from most people and I liked her the more for it. She had a translucent quality — an ability to walk through a room full of people as though she were the only one there. At times I felt she could pass right through me and never know it, waft around me like scented air. At the time of the fire, she was in her mid-20s, small and easily overlooked, with long dark hair that she wore in a single loose braid down her back — most definitely not the style at the time. All of her clothes had a well-washed look, as though they had already been worn out by someone else, and even in summer, she wore a pair of shabby cotton lady's gloves in ivory or pale pink, the kind usually reserved for proms, with fingertips grey from use. She looked vaguely foreign, although there was no telling from where — just that she hadn't come from the world she was living in.

After some time, Uncle Jesse didn't want to wait anymore for the verdict from the officials, so he filled his rucksack and left for good without so much as a nod toward me. With him gone, all living evidence of the summer had vanished. If I'd known how to get there, I would have ridden my bike to Hermitage Street and stood in the backyard of the burnt house with whatever was left of Aunt Charlotte's garden, just to be sure I hadn't made the whole thing up.

MY MOTHER HAD A TALENT FOR CREATING NORMALCY where there was no right to it, and so it wasn't long before my time with Aunt Charlotte took on the status of a dream — but that didn't mean anything about the hole she left behind. It felt like a keyhole, black and cool, with different air on the other side: the air she would breathe. Maybe the breeze held a bit of heat that had come from her lips as she slept. Imagining made it so, but it still wasn't the same as being in the hammock where the air was saturated with her, seeing as it had rubbed up against her insides over and over, and up against mine. To share the same air — that can't be replaced.

All that time with Aunt Charlotte in her garden had given me a taste for wildness. Now with her gone, I gravitated to the manicured cemetery down the street from my family house, where the trees towered. I clutched at the tiny islands of wildness along the edge of that cemetery — the places where the mower didn't go, where a half-dozen trees might stand together and make something that to me was more holy than a temple. In those places, seeds were planted by the wind — the fingers of God.

Sometimes I'd imagine how those islands could be made larger. If I scattered those seeds just right and watered them, they could expand inch by inch until they met other islands of trees. Then those islands would meet the trees that lined the streets and there would be a continuous forest. But when I looked around, I knew it wasn't possible. Not with all the fences around people's yards, the manicured lawn of the cemetery. They'd pull those little saplings out like weeds. But maybe someday all the fences would be gone, the lawns would become meadows, and someone like Aunt

Charlotte would come and be able to make a forest again. I thought about that a lot, lying on the ground in those tiny stands of trees at the edge of the cemetery.

In time, I came to see the "Char" in Aunt Charlotte's name as an obvious omen. She was Charred-Lata, whereas I was thankfully just Lata — Lata Marie. I took comfort in this, until it finally dawned on me that the omens were just as obvious in my name. After all, I was named for her. And while my first name got hung on the infant of me by my mother's love for her baby sister, the second, Mom said she chose because it sounded good. Her explanation never fooled me. None of us know on the surface what we're really doing. We use logic to explain mystery and then say the things we made up as though they're true.

Here's the real truth: my fate hung on the pleasing ring of Marie beside Lata — it was my main inheritance, the doorway where the spirits could enter, for Marie was not only the hidden middle name of my mother, my grandmother and my great grandmother, it was also the given name of my great Aunt Marie. Aunt Charlotte once told me that to be given the name meant that Aunt Marie had sent her spirit back to help, and she lived and breathed in me. She often spoke as though I already knew the things Marie had told her. Maybe that's why I wasn't surprised when it turned out to be true that the knowings came to me in ways other than the usual.

2

THE HOUSE ON HERMITAGE STREET

Lata

ALTHOUGH AUNT CHARLOTTE always had a special fondness for me, what with me being named for her, I didn't spend any real time with her until the summer I turned eight, after Grandma Emmie had her stroke. At that time, my mother had her hands full with my seven brothers and sisters, the youngest being two, and on top of that, Grandma's sickness. Then my father hurt his back, and when Mom found out he'd be laid up for a couple of months, she started farming out the younger kids, including me, and I started spending long weekends with Aunt Charlotte and Uncle Jesse in their house on Hermitage Street.

Uncle Jesse loved that house. It was set back on an exceptionally large lot that covered more than half a city block. A white picket fence bordered the front yard, meeting a taller, plank fence at the side of the house that circled the rest of the property. The picket tops were so perfectly oval that from the upstairs window, the fence looked like it was made of popsicle sticks. Beyond the fence I could see Mrs. Petty's house, which was a small bungalow, as were most of the nearly identical buildings on the block, built in the 20s for factory workers and covered with grey asbestos siding. Only Uncle Jesse's house was different. A rambling Victorian with a turret and a wrap-around porch, he told me it had once been the grand summer home of a prominent politician, originally built on the outskirts of the city. Much later, the neighborhood grew up around it. Years of neglect had made it affordable and Uncle Jesse was fixing it up.

When I was visiting, I often woke to the sound of hammers and power saws and the smell of paint or spackle or freshly-cut wood. Uncle Jesse worked carefully in small, contained areas of the house whenever possible, as though renovation could happen without disruption. I liked to watch him work. Sometimes I held a little pile of nails in my cupped hands and he'd dig out the proper one with his big fingers. I wanted to stand close to him and feel the heat that came from his constant motion. I liked the way the muscles of his arms worked, the assured way he tore out rotted wood and replaced it with fresh two-by-fours. He acted like he could fix anything, as though he knew in an instant what was broken and what was whole.

When he wasn't working on the house or at the construction site, Uncle Jesse liked to spend his free time at garage sales in search of Victorian doorknobs to replace the broken ones, or sifting through tangles of discarded junk for things he could restore. My first Sunday there, he took me with him and I dug through boxes of rusted metal looking for something that would please him. I found an old door knocker with a lion's head holding a ring in its mouth. Uncle Jesse was so happy he tossed me into the air, like they do in the movies.

We went together often after that and he always asked Aunt Charlotte to come along. "Treasure hunting?" he'd say, as if he'd never said it before. I don't know why he kept asking. She never wanted to go and the invitation immediately made her turn grey. How could he not notice? Seems he thought he could renovate her too — that if he kept at it long enough, she'd respond just as he liked. But Aunt Charlotte never seemed to pay attention to the usual things. She didn't shop or watch TV, barely read the newspaper and she hardly ever talked. She liked to go to the tiny strip of forest preserve near the railroad tracks to look for lichen-covered sticks and little plants with red berries that she could plant in the backyard. She and I went there together, though Uncle Jesse wasn't happy about it. He said you weren't supposed to take plants from the forest preserve. Besides, high school boys went there to get drunk and make trouble. It was no place for a woman and a child. He offered to take us to the nursery where Aunt Charlotte could buy proper flowers for the garden, but she refused.

The garden was the only thing Aunt Charlotte took any interest in, but Uncle Jesse wouldn't let her be in charge of the front of the house where people could see. Her taste was too wild and unkempt, he said. It didn't go with the house. But in the back, Aunt Charlotte did as she pleased. The only plants she bought from the nursery were hyacinth bulbs and starter herbs that she used for tea: mint, chamomile, feverfew and lavender. All of the other plants came either from trips to the forest preserve or from the vacant lot at the end of the block. Some, she said, came from the corridor of wild grasses where the trains ran, but she never took me there.

Others would call them weeds, but Aunt Charlotte nurtured her plants the way Mrs. Petty nurtured her African violets. I helped her plant clusters of goldenseal, columbine and bloodroot in the bare earth between the old oak and the baby cedar tree that Uncle Jesse had gotten for her when they first moved in. There were other plants coming up by themselves that she had planted before I came. Many were so plain looking that most people wouldn't think of putting them in a garden, but Aunt Charlotte said all of them had secret gifts if only you knew how to look. Sometimes the secret was in the berry, how it would dye old linen napkins a subtle shade of plum. Sometimes it was in the leaves, how their tea would cool a fever or soothe a raspy throat. Some of the plants were for the birds, like the little patch of thistles she put in for the finches. Other plants were for the butterflies, like the milkweed that Uncle Jesse made clear he disliked. Then there were the sticks with a few ragged leaves attached that Aunt Charlotte assured me would one day be trees. She said these were the plants that really belonged in the yard: they had been there long before the house, when the land was still prairie and forest.

It was late spring when the garden began to creep out from the backyard. Uncle Jesse didn't like it and he let her know. Aunt Charlotte didn't say anything when he complained, but she didn't stop planting things, either. She told me that plants knew where they belonged. Some of them belonged in the backyard, but some of them needed to be in the front. It wasn't really up to her. It was up to them.

AFTER SCHOOL LET OUT, the weekends on Hermitage Street began to stretch into weeks, now that my mother was sure I didn't mind. Truth was, I preferred being there to being at home, where I often felt trampled by the chaotic energy of my brothers and sisters, not to mention my mother's stress at all the caring she had to do, what with my father's back still hurting and Grandma Emmie still needing lots of help. On Hermitage Street, things were quieter and moved at a pace that made sense to me.

Now that it was summer, Uncle Jesse spent long hours at the construction site. At first I missed his attention and our trips to the garage sales, but I soon forgot about that when I discovered how magical the world could get when Aunt Charlotte had the space and quiet to spread herself out without the sound of Uncle Jesse's hammers and saws always in the background. We spent most of our time tending the garden, and the yard got more and more like a meadow. We never talked much, but I didn't mind. Instead, we'd hum together this strange, lilting melody that Aunt Charlotte always seemed to have under her breath. It turned the world into a dream space. I felt right at home, digging in the dirt with her, humming in the magic.

One Saturday, Uncle Jesse had the day off and was fixing the front steps while Aunt Charlotte and I went to the park for the afternoon. We came home through the alley to the back gate and found the yarrow she had planted by the front porch piled in a heap by the trash. Aunt Charlotte dropped her purse and gathered the limp plants into her arms like a baby, whispering to them what sounded like apologies, and carried them to the backyard. I brought her purse in for her, then went around to the front and saw that Uncle Jesse had planted climbing rose bushes in their place.

Aunt Charlotte didn't answer when Uncle Jesse called her in for dinner. She stayed in the backyard late into the night. After I had gone to bed, I heard her come in. They were talking in the kitchen, and I crept out of my room and sat at the top of the stairs to listen.

"All I did was pull some weeds," I heard Uncle Jesse say.

"You know I planted that yarrow."

"You can have as much of it as you want in the back yard. We agreed to that. But I don't want the front of the house looking like a vacant lot."

I felt Aunt Charlotte, then — her pain in my belly. The tension between them was dangerous, as though they had come upon a deep canyon with a sudden drop, its edge murky in the darkness.

"I'm making a beautiful house for you. Why can't you be grateful?"

"I don't want a beautiful house," Aunt Charlotte said flatly.

"Then what the hell do you want? Do you want to live in a hovel somewhere in the forest? Like your Aunt Marie? Is that what you want?"

"It's not about what I want. It's about the plants. The trees. The people who come after us. Why do you only talk about wanting?"

I heard a door slam and someone on the stairs, so I ran back in my room and closed the door.

I SLEPT RESTLESSLY and got up just after dawn, anxious to see what Aunt Charlotte had done with the yarrow. The yard was eerie in the morning light. There was no doubt which were the plants she had rescued. Every one of them was wilted and it was clear to me they weren't going to survive. This frightened me. I didn't want to think about what Aunt Charlotte would feel when she saw the plants and what she might say to Uncle Jesse. Years later, I learned that yarrow was used by shamans to protect those who were about to walk on hot coals or otherwise be exposed to great heat, and that the aroma of smoldering yarrow could ward off dark spirits. Even now, far-fetched as it might seem, I can't help ponder what might have been different had Uncle Jesse allowed the yarrow to keep its circle of protection around the house.

I walked around to the front of the house looking for the watering can and noticed a crude sign stuck into the ground across the street. It was advertising a three-family garage sale a few blocks from the house. I ran back to tell Uncle Jesse, but found only Aunt Charlotte in the kitchen, pouring tea. I told her about the sale and was surprised when she put down her cup and said we would go together.

The sale sprawled halfway down the alley. I picked through a box of naked dolls whose hair stuck up straight and fingered the plastic pieces that went with some game long ago discarded. Meanwhile, Aunt Charlotte gathered things to transform: a rickety table for the front hallway that she told me Uncle Jesse would like, a Victorian floor lamp with a milk glass shade and a frayed cord, and three faded linen tablecloths. Later that day, she stirred the tablecloths in a boiling pot and then removed them — now the color of ripe apricots — and draped them, still wet, over the curtain rods in the living room. A part of me was still anxious. I kept waiting for her to go to the backyard, but she seemed to have forgotten about the plants. We sat on the living room floor together, each like cats in our own square of sunlight, and watched the sun filter through the new curtains.

Even though Uncle Jesse's boots were always dirty, he never forgot to wipe his feet. Each night when he came home from the construction site, I'd hear the scrape of his thick soles on the jute mat. Two sets of three scrapes if it was sunny, three sets of four scrapes if it was muddy or raining. That night he did his sunny routine, and then the door thudded open and in he came, smelling like sunlight and sawdust and sweat, his tool belt clanking against his thigh.

Aunt Charlotte went to him immediately, wrapped both arms around his neck and planted kisses in circles on his cheek. For a brief moment, she seemed solid. I could tell that Uncle Jesse was startled and pleased by this. He pressed the back of her hand to his lips. Years ago, she had lost the ring finger of her left hand to frostbite. Just a stub was left, below where the knuckle would have been. That's where Uncle Jesse kissed her: right below the empty space. But Aunt Charlotte's solidity was just smoke gathered into a form that looked real. One puff of air could give it a new shape, and so even though it seemed that she had made up with Uncle Jesse, that all changed the following day.

As Uncle Jesse stripped the banister in the front hallway, Aunt Charlotte and I helped him by taping paint chips to the walls so we could make our choice of color. He wanted to leave them there while he worked so he could watch how the colors changed as the sun arched over the house from day into evening. We worked quickly and then retreated to the front porch away from the chemical fumes, leaving Uncle Jesse to study the paint chips. "I'm betting on the sienna suede," he called to us. Even from the porch I could hear him whistling. I liked hearing him so happy.

Aunt Charlotte and I sat on a rusted metal glider and I flipped through catalogs that Uncle Jesse had saved, the corners turned back on pages with the things he would order just as soon as they had the money: rugs with thick, wool pile and busy jubilant colors, shimmery curtains the color of corn silk, black iron garden chairs with sculptured ivy twining up their legs, a stone planter with lions' faces carved into the bowl. In one catalog I found a cricket cage made of bamboo that looked like a little house with a peaked roof. A cricket sat inside watching itself in a framed mirror. I thrust the catalog into her lap.

"You should get this little house," I said.

"That's not a house, it's a cage."

"It's a house, Aunt Charlotte. Look, it has a little door."

"The cricket can't open the door."

"Maybe she can."

Aunt Charlotte let the catalog slip from her lap and looked up. Across the street, Mrs. Petty hovered in her front window, peering from behind a film of dull white curtains, then disappeared into the shadows. Her jerky movements reminded me of a honeybee.

I felt a shift in the air. I closed the catalog and set it

aside, then wrapped my arms around Aunt Charlotte's waist and laid my head in her lap. Though it was summer, she seemed to be shivering. I sensed that in this moment, she could easily shatter, as though her bones were made of milk glass. She was wearing an old pair of white ladies gloves as she often did and had stuffed the empty finger with cotton balls. I took her hand and pressed the fake finger like a tiny pillow against my palm. She stared into the air, as though she were seeing something essential that was invisible to me.

"Crickets belong outside. Not in a cage," Aunt Charlotte said.

She pulled her hand from mine, gathered up the catalogs and carried them to the trash behind the house. They landed with a thud at the bottom of the can. She walked back swinging her arms as though some great burden had been lifted, and went past me through the front door. I followed her and watched as she tore the paint chips from the walls and balled them in her hand. Uncle Jesse stopped his work on the banister. He held a brush thick with paint stripper straight up, the way you would hold a torch.

"Charlotte, what's gotten into you?"

When she passed Uncle Jesse, he grabbed her arm. "What the hell has come over you?"

"We've done enough," she said. "We've got to stop."

"What're you talking about?"

"This is no way to live. It's crazy. It's all about the house." Aunt Charlotte's eyes got small and bright. "You'd kill for it."

"I have no idea what you're talking about." I'd never

seen him look so scared.

"You killed the yarrow like it was nothing."

Uncle Jesse's face went dark. "Are we back to that again?"

Suddenly, it was as though all the air left her and her arms went limp. The fumes from the paint remover made my eyes burn. I rubbed them with the back of my hands.

Uncle Jesse dropped the paintbrush onto the tarp and reached for Aunt Charlotte. At first she leaned against him out of courtesy, but then she pulled away and took in a breath so strong and deep, she might have been saving herself from drowning.

"I'm going for a walk," she said, and she pushed open the screen door so hard it banged twice behind her. She seemed suddenly large and muscled, as though she could knock down anyone in her path. I watched her disappear down the front steps into the leafy shade of the street. Uncle Jesse watched, too. I could tell from his face that he was seeing her the same way I was.

This was not smoke. It was real change, like a building hit again and again by a wrecking ball, hairline cracks invisible, suddenly crumbling all at once. I found this frightening and thrilling. From the moment she left Uncle Jesse on the porch, I watched Aunt Charlotte with an eager attentiveness. That night I listened for her even as I slept. I thought I heard her leave the house, but when I went to check she was asleep beside Uncle Jesse. Later, I heard her leave again and found her kneeling in the garden. I could see only her white gloves gathering chamomile flowers in the darkness.

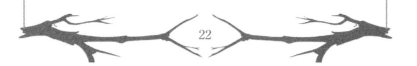

3

MY SECRET WAYS

Charlotte

No one knew about my secret ways. I had ways of knowing that didn't involve the eyes and ears. This felt normal when I was alone in the woods or with Aunt Marie, but at home I kept it to myself. No one told me I had to do this, but people say truth in other ways than words. Ma may have been the one whose arms I laid in as a baby — and I loved her more than anyone — but we both knew Marie was the one who held my soul. I still wanted to anchor in the spacious warmth of her, but she sent me back to the city and the pinched silence of my parent's house. Sometimes I heard her voice thrumming in the leaves of the apple tree outside my bedroom window. *Posoh, little one, posoh.* She spoke to me in the old language words I didn't understand.

A few months after I'd left her forest, Aunt Marie's spirit brought me to St. Francis woods for the first time. In the backyard, the leaves of the apple tree were falling, brittle and tan. Sitting against the trunk as I often did, mind soaked through and stilled by the loss of her, wind settling the leaves into a rustling border around the garage, I heard a humming so faint I couldn't tell if it was really there. It seemed to move through the trees. I went out front to where the elms formed a grand arc down the street, dwarfing the frame bungalows with their square front lawns. The sound amplified, then disappeared, and I walked close to the elms, listening.

I followed that sound to the main road that Ma didn't like me to cross, passed Kresge's drugstore where Pa sometimes brought us to get Cokes at the counter; passed the shoemaker's window with its hand-lettered sign and rows of dusty abandoned shoes; through the clouds of starch wafting from the commercial laundry. I followed it across a busy intersection to a mass of trees held in by a long stretch of black iron fence and walked a city block until I came to a gate with an engraved metal sign: Convent of the Sisters of Saint Francis. I slipped inside and walked the concrete path until it curved behind the chapel onto a trail in a dense forest I never knew was there.

When my foot left the concrete and touched the bare earth, something in me let go until my body felt so light, I thought I could be lifted by the wind. I walked the dirt path through maples and oaks and before long, came to a clearing where an outcropping of rocks had been turned into a grotto for a painted statue of the Blessed Virgin, tall as a grown woman, her blue gown billowing at her feet, painted eyes half closed in an expression that mixed rapture with heartbreak. I sat under a clump of white birch facing the statue and closed my eyes. There I could recognize the music: it was Marie's voice humming the melody she had sung to me by the river. I went inside the song and rested

there as sure as if I were sleeping with my head in Aunt Marie's lap.

Maybe I really did fall asleep because next thing I knew, the air felt cool and the forest was silent. I felt a presence I didn't recognize — the sense of someone small and scared ducking behind the grotto. I followed it down a narrow path to the clearing where the Sisters of St Francis buried their nuns in rows as straight and even as school desks. Some of the graves had sunk crooked into the earth. I walked between the rows, feeling the frightened presence move with the wind as I read the names, so foreign to me: Helga and Buela, Marta and Gustafie. Why were they so far from home? I could feel their loneliness prickling the air. Fear and sadness churned between the gravestones and turned to sickness in my stomach. The feeling was strongest beside Gustafie's grave. I knelt there and whispered, *it's okay, it's okay, it's okay, it's okay,* over and over, until I wasn't saying words anymore, just the rhythm of a heartbeat, steady and sure.

IT WAS DARK BY THE TIME I GOT HOME. The reading lamp beside Pa's chair glowed through the sheer curtains that covered the living room windows, so I went around to the kitchen door. I could see Ma through the window cutting carrots by the stove. She looked inviting in her blue flowered work dress, greying hair brushing the collar, calves sturdy and reassuring, a white apron tied around her thick waist. When I opened the door, she turned abruptly. A smear of white powder dusted her cheek and made her dark eyes appear even darker. She must have made biscuits.

"I've been worried sick about you," she said in a low voice stern with fear. "Where've you been?"

She put the knife on the counter and plucked a brown pine needle from my hair. I couldn't lie to her. "I went to the woods behind the convent."

Ma looked confused. "I've never taken you there. How did you know where to go?"

"Aunt Marie showed me."

Ma's eyes went wet. She looked away, and then plucked a twig from my sweater. "You be careful from now on. Cross with the light. And be back before your Pa gets home."

ALL OF US MOVED AROUND PA with great care, as you would around a sleeping bear. He never said much, but when he did, his words weighed more than anyone's. Some of them were so heavy they could break your foot if you dropped them, so we listened close, scared we might get hurt. I can't say exactly why. Pa was careful in his movements, never sudden or aggressive. He never hit me or my older sister Belle, and he certainly never hit Ma. When we sat at the square wooden table in the kitchen for dinner, I'd often watch how his eyes followed Ma's hands as she dished up plates of beef stew and potatoes. Just by looking at her, the worried lines on his face would soften as though her silent presence spread salve on his hurts. Maybe she knew a secret we didn't, and our care around Pa prevented a disaster I'll never know.

I kept out of his way, but Belle worked anxiously to please him, getting straight A's and learning to bake. She was 14 years older than me and thought she would always

be the only one, seeing as Ma and Pa married later in life than was usual. She looked just right in her red lipstick and ladies suits, high-heeled shoes showing off her pretty calves, dark hair curled in the latest style. How easily she attracted a handsome soldier from an upright German family — smart, funny and kind — released from his duties in army intelligence after the big victory. They married a month after she turned 21, with me as her flower girl. Pa approved of her choices with a grunt and a nod — some-times even a wink and a smile — and that's how I knew Belle belonged to him.

But not me. I belonged to Aunt Marie. I have Ma to thank for that. She saw that I couldn't belong to Pa the way Belle did. I was a dreamer and needed a guide. Aunt Marie was older than Ma and didn't go to the government board-ing school to learn from the nuns like Ma and her other sisters did. She still had a foot in the old way and knew something about these things, so one summer, Ma brought me to the reservation and left me with her while she and Belle visited the rest of the family.

Ma's other sisters didn't approve of Aunt Marie. They said she was backward and drank too much. Though she was supposed to be Catholic, she hardly ever went to church and she made no secret that she still practiced some of the old ways. Belle told me that except for Marie, Ma's sisters all permed their dark hair so it went lighter. They considered themselves French Catholics and pretended they had no Indian blood at all, but Aunt Marie told me they had Menominee, Mohawk, Mascoutin and Ottawa — and so did I. Much later, I learned Ma's sisters had good reason to pretend. In that government boarding school, it wasn't safe to claim Menominee blood — not with what could happen. One girl had boiling water poured on her back just for speaking Menominee to her friend on the first day of school, before she'd learned any English. Hard to think of Ma at age 10, forced to spend eight years in such a place.

Even though he barely knew them, Pa didn't approve of anyone on the reservation. When Ma first told him she wanted to take us for a visit, he forbid her to go. That was one of the few times I ever saw Ma stand up to him. She clipped coupons and saved pennies from her grocery money until she had enough for three train tickets to Green Bay and bus tickets to Shawano. He finally agreed to drive us to the train station, and Grandpa Abe picked us up once we arrived in Green Bay.

After that trip, Ma never took me back to that forest. For a long time, I didn't even know how to find it on a map. Maybe that's why Aunt Marie showed me the way to St. Francis woods. I found a home in those trees. Pa never knew. He would have put a stop to it, so I learned to know by the sky when I had to leave for home.

The woods taught me things you can't learn from people, like how to make friends with trees and the little plants that grow beneath them. I gave nicknames to my favorites: Shy Apple, Fancy Leaves, Moon Petal and Invisible Grass, and learned what time of year I could expect them, when they'd bloom, how much sun would dry them up. I made friends with the birds, too. I named them Grey Baby, Brown Belly, and Blue Holler Mouth. I tried to learn their language by imitating their sounds, and sometimes they talked back, but I never could understand much of what they were saying.

Often I would feel the spirits of the nuns milling around the graveyard. They all blended together and I couldn't tell one from another, except for Gustafie. She was the only one who would venture away from the graveyard toward the grotto and sometimes she followed me to the meadow or into the pines. Over time we got used to each other, and even though we didn't talk, I spent more time in her presence when I was growing up than with any living person.

When children make friends with spirits, people call them imaginary friends. Seems to me it's a trick, so they'll question their own knowing. It didn't happen that way for me. Ma never used the word "imaginary." She didn't spend much time with them herself, but she knew those spirits were as real as you and me.

Once in a while, one of my teachers would call Ma in for a talk and tell her how something wasn't right with me and I shouldn't spend so much time alone. I knew because that's when Ma would tell me to go visit Anita Chakowski next door, even though she knew Anita laughed too loud and screamed at every little bug. Luckily, Ma never pushed. Had there been someone suitable, she knew I would have happily had a friend.

Pa didn't push, either. It was normal to him, that I was alone. That's how he was. He only loved Ma. Why would anyone need more than that? But as I got older, I knew Ma worried, seeing as the world doesn't take kindly to someone peculiar. "In another time and place she would have been fine as she is," I once heard her say to Belle. "But

I don't know how she'll get on in this one."

IT WAS MA'S CONCERN that got me to Aunt Marie, and for that I'm grateful. We took a train there the year I turned 10, along with Belle, and reached Green Bay under a dull aluminum sky. Ma and Belle struggled with the two suitcases while I carried a cardboard box filled with a half a dozen jars of homemade strawberry-rhubarb jam to give as gifts. Ma pointed me toward Grandpa Abe, who leaned against a pillar near the station door smoking his pipe, the buttons of his old pinstripe vest pulled tight over his round belly, heavy boots caked with mud brushing the cuffs of his gentleman pants. He took his time finishing up his smoke before he walked toward us.

"Thought I'd make it easy on you and save you the bus trip," Grandpa said, patting Ma on the arm. She nodded gratefully, and he turned to Belle.

"Aren't you the lady," he said, nodding toward her pressed red dress with its skinny black belt. He took the suitcase from her hand. Belle smiled and started to say something, but he'd already stepped toward me. His sleeve brushed against my cheek. It smelled of stale pipe tobacco and manure.

"I thought you was still knee high," he said, his long mustache wiggling as he spoke. "You coming with us, then, to see your aunties?"

"Best we drop her with Marie before heading for the farm," Ma said to Grandpa, "and keep it quiet. If they know she's staying with Marie, the whole visit will turn sour from the get-go."

Grandpa nodded. He took both suitcases and headed toward the car, a dusty blue Chevy with a loose bumper. As he opened the front door for Ma, me and Belle climbed in back onto the sticky vinyl seat.

From Green Bay to the reservation, I watched the open farm fields and nondescript buildings pass by. Grandpa Abe had the radio tuned to a ball game that came in and out from the static, and I could hear the click of Ma's knitting needles. Nobody said much. Belle dug through her purse and pulled out an emery board, and I watched her file her nails into perfect ovals. When she finished, she held them out to check her work, and I held my hands up next to hers.

"Honestly Charlotte," Belle said, "You look like you've come straight from digging in the strawberry patch. You don't want to show up for a visit with lines of dirt under your nails. Scootch over and give me your hand."

I slid toward her on the vinyl seat and Belle took my hand. I closed my eyes and let my attention go to the place where our skin touched, and my fingers became five little baby mice being rocked to sleep. When she finished, Belle coated my hands in rose-scented lotion that made the rest of my skin feel itchy in comparison. Once it soaked in, I held my fingers under my nose to drink in the fragrance.

I was still smelling my hands when we crossed into the reservation. Suddenly we were on a dirt road that cut into an immense stand of trees, the undergrowth thick and healthy, the sunlight tinted green through the leaves. I rolled down my window all the way so I could feel the air on my face, and so did Ma. By then, the radio had gone to pure static, so Grandpa turned it off, and I could hear the buzz of insects and the steady caw of a raven.

"Not much changed since you been here last," Grandpa Abe said to Ma, "except more are moving on to find work. Lumber business been down these past years. Can't compete with them big guys in the north felling trees like they's hay."

We turned down a road that was more like two ruts in the forest floor. The car bounced and heaved over the hard dirt, and in some places, bushes scraped against the doors. I stuck my hand out to pluck a leaf, tore it in half and sniffed it. It smelled faintly like cucumber. A fly buzzed up against the windshield in front of Ma.

"Don't remember this road," Ma said, brushing away the fly.

"A shortcut, if it don't take off the muffler," said Grandpa Abe.

The car emerged in a field so bright that all of us shaded our eyes at the same time. At the far end of the field, a little wooden farmhouse sat crooked on the dusty ground, white cotton curtains billowing out of the windows. Grandpa Abe pulled onto a narrow road that led toward the farmhouse and stopped the engine in a clearing on the side of the road.

"The place looks different," Ma said. "Can't say how."

"We cleared out all those rusted farm tools — the Greschen boys oiled them up for their Mama's field, so she could get a little money selling hay," Grandpa Abe said. "Gave Marie a good spot for a kitchen garden."

Ma nodded with approval. As we unloaded the car, I looked toward the tangle of herbs and orange flowers next

to the porch. The flowers seem to grow and shrink all on their own. Then I saw they weren't flowers at all, but a swarm of monarch butterflies. I ran ahead of everyone onto the narrow garden path, right into their orange cloud. They rose up around me, brushing my face and bare arms with their wings, landing on my fingers and in my hair.

I felt someone brush up against me, light and easy, and heard a laugh that seemed to come up out of the earth. It was Aunt Marie, head thrown back, silver braid swinging, butterflies covering her face. All shyness evaporated. I grabbed her hand and swung. The butterflies swarmed up in a fiery orange flame and landed in the poplars. We stood there together, watching. Though she was barely taller than me, I felt her body as a tree. I didn't feel shy at all until she talked.

"Well, well. Isn't that some hostess gift," Marie said, her voice slow and thick, like honey.

I wanted to answer, but my voice stayed locked inside. Marie squeezed my hand. Ma, Belle and Grandpa Abe were beside us now, and Aunt Marie stood apart from them, even as Grandpa Abe handed her a pair of small towels that my Grandma Sarah had embroidered before she died.

"Thought you might get some use out of these," Grandpa said. "Old guy like me don't need the likes of them to wipe his hands."

Marie took the towels, but they seemed as strange in her hands as in Grandpa's. Watching Marie, so rooted in her place, so far from the others, I felt suddenly foreign and thought with longing of the apple tree in our backyard — how well I knew it, like a sister. Now I stood on a barren farm, a little garden pressing up against a dry field of tall grass, poplars crooked and lonely. A house of sorrow. I could feel it, as though the windows might weep, and I didn't want to go inside.

Grandpa Abe walked to the front porch and lit his pipe. Ma stood on the footpath with Marie and they held each other's hands, nodding solemnly, a greeting I'd never seen her use with anyone else.

"Run back to the car, Charlotte, and get a couple of jars of jam for your Aunt Marie," Ma said without turning her head.

I took my time, brushing my hand over a clump of yarrow, plucking a fuzzy mullein leaf to roll between my fingers and sniff. By the time I got back, the adults were inside the house and I could hear their voices through the screen door. I pushed it open with my foot and stepped into the kitchen. Ma, Belle and Grandpa sat at a rickety wooden table, uncomfortable in spindle back chairs, as Marie poured hot water into chipped blue cups with Lipton tea bags hanging over their sides. The inside of the house had air so thick with memory I thought I would choke. I put the jelly jars on the table and before Ma could say anything, went back out to the garden, the screen door slamming behind me. Then Grandpa came out, lit his pipe and headed for the car. Belle followed soon after. Ma stopped on the porch and again held both of Marie's hands as she spoke to her in a low voice.

"Charlotte?" Ma called. I was crouching at the edge of the porch watching a bee poke at the yarrow. "You do as Aunt Marie says and don't go wandering off without asking first, you hear?"

I stood up then, and grabbed Ma's sleeve. I didn't want her to leave. Something about Aunt Marie and the sad little house made me uneasy.

"Aunt Marie hasn't been feeling well, so do what you can to help." Ma gave my shoulder a squeeze, then walked down the path to the car and climbed in. The wheels left a cloud of brown dust.

With just the two of us on the porch, I felt in Aunt Marie a wide-open space. Just like Ma, she would not insist on anything. But then a shadow passed over her eyes and she coughed. Her throat made an ugly, raspy sound, and I needed to get away. She didn't stop me from moving through the tall grass to the river's edge where the gnats hummed in grey clouds and the sun hung low in the trees. I crouched on the riverbank and sifted the pebbles between my fingers in an endless, circular movement, listening to their faint rhythms.

I got lost in those stones, I suppose, because before I knew it, the sun had dropped below the horizon and the world was suddenly dark. As my eyes adjusted, I could see shards of blackness moving through the twilight and thought I heard the murmur of voices. Startled, I dropped the stones and glanced over my shoulder toward the dim light of the house. It looked small and far away. Then I noticed Marie crouching a few feet away from me looking into the water, a shadow in the dusk. I breathed in relief. I hadn't heard her come, but still it felt natural, as though we had always crouched together in the dark by the river's edge. Together we watched the moon rise and lay its reflection on the water. Marie took something from her pocket and scattered it. Then she started humming a simple melody that somehow untangled a thread in me and left a raw place where a knot of fear had been. My eyes filled up.

"Them ghosts gather near one like you," Marie said in that slow way she had, as though she were tasting every word. "It's not easy. You need a sword in your heart to know all their sorrow and not make it yours. Not always so good at it myself."

4

MAKING
MEDICINE

Charlotte

AUNT MARIE LET ME SLEEP on the porch on a pile of wool blankets, and I woke with the first bird. Soon, I heard the floor creak from inside the house. I opened the screen door and sat at the rickety table where the blue cups from the day before still lingered, the tea bags dried into wads. Two cabinets hung crooked near the sink, the undersides brown with grease. Aunt Marie stood at the counter sipping coffee from a cracked mug the color of mud, stopping only to sweeten it with whiskey from a dented silver flask.

"Only thing seems to get me oiled up for the day," she said, and winked.

The counter was cluttered with stacks of papers, empty jelly jars and piles of dried herbs, some tied into bundles with twine. A pot boiled on the wood stove, its pungent smell laced with licorice. Aunt Marie took a handful of herbs and broke them into the pot, tinging the smell with a sickly sweetness.

"What're you making?" I asked.

"Medicine," Marie said, stirring. "Smells nasty, I know. Smells worse when I got all I need for it. Run out of a few things. Let's hope it still does the job." She covered the pot, then took a jelly jar from the counter and carried it to the sink. "Get yourself an apple and some of that bread on the table if you're hungry," she said, turning on the faucet. It sputtered rust, then ran clear.

I watched Marie's elbow vibrate as she scrubbed the jar with a bottle brush. Then she coughed and the vigor left her. Anyone could choke on air so thick, a room so dim. I squeezed my eyes shut to keep it from getting inside.

When I opened my eyes again, I was alone in the kitchen. A square of sunlight illuminated a bundle of herbs and beside it, Marie's coffee cup. Just a little was left in the bottom. I took a sip. Not at all like Ma's coffee — Marie's was thick as syrup, with a bitter, mysterious taste full of fire. I turned on the tap and lapped water like a dog. Through the window over the sink, I could see Marie in the garden, a small pipe dangling from her mouth.

I went outside to where Marie was kneeling, harvesting carrots. She reached into her pocket for a pinch of something that she sprinkled around the base of the plant before digging it up and placing it on a newspaper. Then she stopped to light her pipe and took a long, slow inhale, holding the smoke inside for a moment. When she blew it out, I noticed it didn't have much of a smell. When Grandpa smoked his pipe, the whole world smelled of it.

"Back's killing me," Marie said. She stood up slow, leaning on her knee. "How about you finish up the carrots?"

I knelt in her place, and Marie handed me a weathered deerskin pouch a little bigger than my hand.

"This here's tobacco," Marie said. "Important you give before you take. Make your prayer of thanks to the earth

41

for her gift of the carrot. Let her know you'll use it to stay healthy and do good. Then sprinkle a little tobacco there as your gift. Never pull up a plant before you do that."

I took a pinch of the tobacco and sniffed it. It smelled just like Grandpa's pipe.

"How come your pipe doesn't smell like this?" I asked.

"I don't smoke the tobacco — just use it for offerings." Marie lit her pipe and held it out. "This here's mullein. Good for the lungs." She inhaled it deeply.

"Grandpa smokes tobacco."

Marie sent out a stream of white smoke. "Lot of folks do. Not a good use of it if you ask me, except in ceremony. Weakens the effect. And it's hard on the lungs."

I looked down at the carrots, the pouch of tobacco in my hand. I thought of Ma bending over the little patch of carrots in the garden at home, pulling them out efficiently, one right after the other.

"Ma never sprinkles tobacco before she pulls up carrots," I said. As the words came out, I felt a twinge of fear, as though I were confessing something terrible.

When Marie spoke, her voice had just the slightest pinched quality. "Your Ma has her own ways of praying, learned from them nuns. This here's the way our grandma taught us." She stepped onto the porch and opened the screen door. "I need to lay down. Bring them in when you have half a dozen."

Marie paused, hand still on the doorknob. "And take your time with them prayers. They ain't prayers unless you mean them."

I did as Marie asked: before each carrot, I whispered a prayer, trying to mean it, then sprinkled tobacco. Ma taught me to thank God for the food before I ate it, but I'd never heard of thanking the earth and giving it gifts. It made sense to me. I pulled out a carrot and in its place, slid my index finger, then packed the dirt around it. Something strangely comforting. I wanted to bury more of myself and feel the earth press into my body. What would it feel like, to be a root, filled with a mystery that nourishes?

From inside the house, the sound of Marie's sleep drifted through the door — snores and wheezes and an occasional gurgle. I sprinkled tobacco around my finger, then slid it out. It felt different from the others — electric like. I dug a hole big enough to bury my whole hand, palm down. I sprinkled tobacco, then patted the earth around it. No, my fingers needed to point down, the way carrots point down. I dug again, intent, working the places where the ground was hard, testing the depth, until I could fit both hands side by side. I packed in my left hand, then slid in my right, using my foot to move the earth.

I looked up. Stragglers from yesterday's cloud of butterflies still fluttered through the garden. I closed my eyes and put all attention into my hands, the earth pressing into them something comforting, something frightening. I wanted to pull them out, but I was afraid. There was no way to make the tobacco offering Marie required. The pouch lay on the ground, too close to reach with my foot. Now the fear came in a rush. I did it all wrong and trapped myself in the earth.

I could hear Pa saying, "Stop with this foolishness and

43

do as you were told. Marie is waiting for the carrots." But I couldn't bring myself to do it: I couldn't pull my hands from the earth without the tobacco offering. My knees started to ache. I tried to take the pressure off, but no amount of adjustment would make me comfortable. The sun was getting high now, and a bead of sweat dripped from my forehead down the side of my nose. What would Marie think when she found me planted in the carrot patch? My back heaved; sobs pushed up from my belly.

I heard the growl of an engine and looked up. An old pickup had stopped on the road, the nose of a black dog sticking out of the passenger window. Fishing rods were mounted between rusty poles behind the cab. The pickup pulled in where Grandpa had parked and went quiet. A man stepped out, carrying a paper sack under one arm. The dog squealed and barked, but the man seemed not to notice. He headed down the path toward the house.

My heart quickened. I bent down further toward the earth, hoping the drift of yarrow on my right would hide me. I could feel the man glance toward me as he walked by, but he didn't stop. I thought of Aunt Marie asleep on the couch. I pulled my hands from the earth and ran to the porch just as the screen door slammed behind him. He stood on the other side of the door, his worn, grey t-shirt blocking my view. A strong, unpleasant smell rose from him, like old bananas.

"*Posoh*, Frank. Wasn't expecting you until later," I heard Aunt Marie say. "Have a seat."

"Got the grains you asked for, and the whiskey. And I brought you some government butter." Frank emptied the bag onto the table.

"Good of you," Marie said, moving toward the counter. "Leave me just a little chunk of the butter. Won't keep in this heat." She poured coffee into two mugs, then handed one to Frank. "How's she doing?"

"Better than last week, but coughing worse at night."

"Give her an extra dose before bed." Marie carried two jam jars filled with a brown syrup to the table. She held out the one she had filled that morning. "Use this one last. Needs a couple of days to sit."

She put the jars into Frank's empty sack, then walked back to the counter, catching my eye through the screen door. "Charlotte, come in and say hello to Frank."

I opened the door and slipped in.

"This here's my niece," said Aunt Marie. "Emmie's girl."

Frank nodded toward me without quite seeing. He looked disheveled and small, hunched over his coffee mug, but I sensed something volatile. I wanted him to leave.

"The baby is starting to cough a bit. Afraid she might got it, too," Frank said into the mug.

"Weren't you going to bring her by your sister?"

"I told you, I ain't giving up my daughter," Frank said, his voice suddenly thick and hard.

"No one said anything about giving her up," Marie said. "Just preventing the sickness."

Frank narrowed his eyes. "I ain't so easy to trick. Don't take me for no fool." He swallowed down the rest of the coffee in one gulp. I was getting scared.

Aunt Marie moved toward the sink, opened the cabinet, and took out a small vial.

"Keep her at home then, if you need to," Marie said. "Give her 10 drops of this under her tongue, morning and night. We'll see if we can't nip it while its small." She handed him the vial.

Frank took it from her and held it in his palm. It seemed to calm him.

"Careful with it. That medicine's hard to come by," Marie said.

"I ain't no fool," Frank said, pushing the chair back hard. He walked past us without a glance. I stood at the screen door next to Aunt Marie and watched him make his way back to his truck.

"Damn right he's a fool," Aunt Marie said under her breath. "Let's hope he gets them drops into her."

AFTER LUNCH, Marie filled a dull plastic bread bag with tobacco. She put it in her pocket and gave me her deerskin pouch. "You'll be needing your own supply," she said. "Could use your help with some gathering."

I fingered the pouch. Part of Marie still lived in its suppleness: I could feel how often the oils in her fingers had touched it. She handed me a worn burlap bag and we headed across the road onto a narrow path in the forest, dim with its thick cover of birch, oak, maple and pine. I had never been in a forest so dense, and I couldn't imagine a place more beautiful. Marie stooped to pick up a pine cone.

"This here's from a balsam fir," Marie said. "You can spot it by the narrow cones, a kind of purple color." She handed me the cone. "The bark is what I need."

Marie made her tobacco offering at the base of the tree.

Then she took a knife from her pocket.

"Take a look," she said. "These little bumps on the bark hold a real treasure." She poked one with the tip of her knife and a golden liquid oozed out. "This here is pitch," she said. "Used for medicine. The underside of the bark is medicine, too."

I put my finger on the blister. The pitch was sticky as glue.

Marie peeled a length of bark from the trunk and put it in the basket. "I'll need more. Best we find it from a different tree. Let me know when you see one."

I skipped ahead on the path, the cone still in my hand, giddy with pride—as though I had been anointed. I would learn where the medicine hides, under the bark and in the roots. I would know the secrets of plants and use them to heal. I thought of Ma, the twitch over her left eye. Maybe there was a cure for that twitch hidden under the forest floor or in the end of a pine needle.

"Will you be keeping that cone?" I heard Marie say. I stopped and turned.

"Fine if you do," Marie said, taking a puff on her pipe. "But then you need to make your prayer to the tree."

I felt a heat rise over my neck. I walked back to the tree and laid the cone at its base, then took a pinch of tobacco from the leather pouch.

"You need to have a good reason to take part of a plant," Marie said. "Now tell the tree what you'll be using that cone for — to help find medicine for your old Aunt Marie so she can heal herself and a few other folks, too."

I knelt at the base of the tree and looked down at my

fingers. In my embarrassment, I found it hard to concentrate. Aunt Marie had walked a little ways up the path.
I took a deep breath and pictured Frank, vial in his palm,
driving his pickup to a house where a baby girl coughed.
I said the prayer again from the center of my chest and
sprinkled my tobacco.

When I stood up, I saw that we didn't need to go
further. There were three other balsam firs right there by
the trail.

"Aunt Marie," I called. "I found three more trees."

Marie took a sip from her flask, then put it back into her
apron pocket. "Good," she said. "I need just that many."

ON THE WAY BACK to the farmhouse, Marie showed me
how to cut boughs from the old cedar and wrap them into
wands for cleansing and smoke offerings.

"She's old, so it's best not to gather too much," Marie
said. "Her medicine is strong. You can take some home
with you."

Later, we sat on the porch to watch the moon rise,
Marie smoking her newly filled pipe. As the light dimmed,
shadows from the trees fell across the field. I felt a cold-
ness that comes from the dead: ancestors whose names no
one remembers. So many in the field. I wanted to ask
Marie why the spirits were always hovering, making you
feel things that weren't yours to feel, but she was dozing
in her chair, flask resting in her lap, breath like the sound
of the wind. I watched the rise and fall of her belly.
Somehow, she just kept breathing it in.

After Marie went to bed, I slept fitfully on the porch.

The night was long and difficult. Each time I fell asleep, Aunt Marie coughed or snored. Each time I woke up, I could see shadows over the fields and shivered with what hovered there. After a while, I couldn't tell if I was actually on the porch, or just dreaming I was there. Finally, I sat up and leaned against the wall of the house, waiting for the sun to rise and for the sound of Aunt Marie. As soon as I heard movement, I went inside.

"Stir the fire for me, little one," Marie said from her place at the counter.

I picked up the poker and pushed down the stove latch with its end. The fire leapt up in a sudden burst and sent a large ember to land on the linoleum floor. I stamped it out with my bare foot.

"Careful," Marie said, walking over to where I stood. "Does it hurt?"

I shook my head. Marie knelt down to look at my foot. "Not a mark," she said, impressed. "You'd think you was Wabeno."

"What's Wabeno?"

"Uses fire for medicine, that one. Can't be burned." Marie stood up. "What'd you dream?"

I shrugged. I didn't know how to explain about the un-realness of the porch.

"Dreams aren't the kind of business you ignore," Aunt Marie said, taking the poker from my hand. "Best you get to work remembering."

AFTER BREAKFAST, we made medicines from what we'd gathered the day before. I scraped the back of the balsam

49

bark into a boiling pot. Meanwhile, Marie mixed the pitch with an oily substance that gave off a ripe odor.

"What's that smell?" I asked.

"Sturgeon oil," Marie said. "Afraid it might be a little rancid."

"What's it for?"

"Mixed with the pitch, I find it makes the strongest medicine for the sickness. Gave mine to Frank yesterday for his little one." I watched Marie pour the mixture into a small bottle that used to hold eye drops. "Let's hope he ain't let it go to waste." Marie shook the bottle, then opened her mouth and dripped the medicine under her tongue.

"Smells fishy," I said.

"Oil comes from a fish. But that's the last you'll smell of it," Marie said. "Impossible to get now. Been a long time since the sturgeon come this way. Used to spawn at Keshena Falls before the dam went in. A special place. Ask your Grandpa Abe to show you tomorrow on the way to the train."

"I'm leaving tomorrow?" I said, feeling a wave of relief. I wanted to get away from the sad house with its ghosts and strange smells. I thought of the apple tree, Ma's biscuits. I looked up at Aunt Marie sipping coffee laced with whiskey from her brown mug, eyes tired and blurry. I didn't want to think about leaving her alone.

Later, we washed the sheets in the river. I hung them on a line strung between two poplars, then sat on a rock and watched them flap in the wind. In the distance I heard the sound of an engine, a dog bark. For a moment, time collapsed, and I thought it might be Grandpa Abe come to get

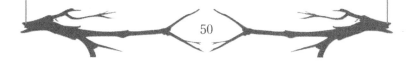

me. But then I remembered — one more night here with Aunt Marie. Already, I felt nostalgic. I walked around to the garden to see if any of the butterflies were still there. Just as I rounded the bend, I heard the screen door slam and saw Frank's pickup parked in the same spot as yesterday.

I went into the house. Aunt Marie stood at the counter, straining the pot of boiled bark into a jar. Over her head, a portrait of Jesus hung crooked, a water stain blurring his body into space. The dusty frond of a dried palm and a braid of sweetgrass lay across the top of the plastic frame. Frank paced between the sink and the table.

"Didn't sleep a wink last night," said Frank. "Coughing fits all night, waking the baby."

"Did you give the drops to the little one?"

"Course I did. Dammit, I ain't no fool," Frank banged his hand on the counter. "What you take me for?"

"Have her sip hot tea with honey if you have it," Marie said. "And give her the syrup every hour until the cough lets up."

Frank leaned both hands on the table and slumped. "Don't know what I'll do if I lose her." His voice was small, like a little boy.

I felt a pain in my chest. Something of Frank had seeped in. I sat on the floor by the stove, eyes wet, blurring. Marie took a deep breath. Then she walked over to Frank and slid something under his hand.

"20 drops under her tongue every two hours until the bottle's gone," Marie said. "We're going to knock this out of her."

Frank stood up, mumbled a thank you, and headed for

the door. I saw, then, what Marie had given him: her own medicine made this morning from the sturgeon oil. All at once, I understood — without the medicine, it would be Aunt Marie who went. The door slammed behind Frank. I could hear his dog barking in the pickup. I ran out after him and just as he started to climb into the cab, I grabbed his arm.

"That's her medicine," I said, breathless. "Aunt Marie needs it."

Frank turned. I could smell the coffee on his breath. He pulled his arm away.

"She just gave it to me," he said.

"It's the last bottle." I looked up at his truck. The lines from his fishing poles swayed in the wind. "She needs sturgeon oil to make more. Can you catch her a sturgeon?"

"Sturgeon?" Frank said. "Don't come this way since the dam was put in. And they're illegal to catch."

"She needs it."

Frank looked at the bottle in his hand, then back at the house. Just then, Aunt Marie stepped onto the porch. "Marie," he called, walking toward her. "This here your last bottle?"

Marie nodded.

"Girl says you need sturgeon. I'll go tonight. Get the Greschen boys to help me. We got a right to them fish. It's in the treaties. Damn if they'll stop me from getting what's rightfully ours."

"Never mind," Marie said. "I got no need of sturgeon."

"Girl says you need it for your medicine."

"She's wrong," Aunt Marie was fierce. "Now get on back to your wife and baby."

Frank looked at me, then back at Marie.

"Get on home, Frank. Never mind the girl. Come back tomorrow and let me know how they are."

Frank nodded and climbed into the cab, then drove a jerky line down the road.

Aunt Marie grabbed my shoulders. "Don't you be saying such things. You could of caused a big heap of trouble."

My eyes filled up. "You gave him your medicine."

"I got other remedies. Don't you go making decisions that aren't yours to make." She let go of my shoulders and turned away. I watched her walk down the path, passed the garden and up onto the porch, silver braid swaying, the dark wind from the fields blowing against her back.

5

SPLAYED

OPEN

Charlotte

I SAT ON THE GROUND by the yarrow facing the farmhouse and stayed there for a long time. My body ached with tiredness. In time, the door swung open and Aunt Marie called to me from the porch, but I couldn't move. It was as though my chest had a weight strapped to it, holding me in place.

Aunt Marie came down the walk, bent down and took my hand. "Come now," she whispered. We walked together into the farmhouse and she led me over to the couch. "Lie down here," she said. She sat down and patted her leg.

I felt shy at first, being so close to her, but still I lay down and rested my head in her lap. When I felt her hand on my shoulder, tender and light, the grief took over. I closed my eyes and it seeped out, drew lines down my neck that dripped into my hair. The grief wrapped around me like cotton batting, suffocating, and I knew why Aunt Marie needed whiskey in her coffee. I could think of nothing but her lost sisters, the sickness spreading all through the community, the ghosts that lingered around her house — even the lost sturgeon, so important for medicine. I wanted to swallow it all for Marie. I had to do something.

I didn't know what.

"Aunt Marie? I can stay here with you."

"Forget about that. Your life is at home with your Ma and Pa."

"You're wrong."

I saw what I needed to do, through all the layers that suffocated. I had to stay. I would hide in the woods when Ma and Grandpa came until they gave up and left without me. I'd wait long enough so that the train would be long gone, then I'd return to Aunt Marie — tell her I got lost. Aunt Marie would be so relieved to have me, she'd call Ma and say, "might as well leave her here a while. No sense sending her back now." Then I would tend the garden so Marie could save her back. I'd crawl through the over-grown areas by the river until I found the place where the sturgeon still swam. I'd think of a way to catch one using a stick and a string. Then I'd gather the pitch from the balsam fir and make bottles and bottles of remedies — enough for Aunt Marie, and Frank's wife and baby, and anyone else who needed it. Aunt Marie would tell me how.

Satisfied, I let my eyes close. I could feel Marie's stomach rise and fall, and the grief began to spread. It floated overhead like a thin layer of rain clouds. I felt myself dissolving, my head and Marie's lap a warm spot in the sun, my feet the cold river behind the house where the sturgeon used to swim. I moved like mist through the planks of the farmhouse walls, over the wide field and beyond where the forest meets the paved road, to the white clapboard house where Ma, Belle and Aunt Ruthie sat at a farm table sipping tea from china cups. I spread out further, all the way down to the city, where Pa sat alone in his favorite chair, feet on the hassock, head nodding in sleep over his rumpled newspaper.

I sent blessings to all of them. I would stay, and the cedar would come back to life, oceans of mullein bloom in the dry field, the butterflies would flutter by the porch steps year round, and Marie would be emptied of grief. I felt a hand on my forehead. Marie lifted my head and before I could stop her, she slipped away, placing a pillow where her lap had been.

I WOKE TO THE SOUND of Belle's heels on the kitchen floor. It was barely dawn, but they had already packed my suitcase and it was sitting next to the door. I lay back on the pillow and turned away, my fingers clawing into the couch. I tuned all my senses to Aunt Marie — the scent of soil and tobacco that never left her fingers, the softness of her lap — but the person who knelt beside me was Belle. I could smell the pink lotion she used on her hands.

"Time to get a move on." Belle scratched the back of my neck as though I were a puppy.

I could hear Grandpa Abe's boots shuffling on the porch. The smoke from his pipe drifted in through the screen door. How could I have slept so long? I should have been in the woods by now. I opened my eyes just a crack and saw that I was still wearing my clothes from yesterday. The screen door slammed. Then a damp washcloth got laid on my forehead.

"Go ahead, now," I heard Aunt Marie say. "You'll feel better if you wash up a little."

I rubbed the cloth over my cheeks. She was right — it revived me — but it also seemed to wash away any possibility of staying.

"I want you to keep that pouch I gave you. And be sure you take a good handful of those cedar wands you done such a good job wrapping. Just don't try and burn them until they dry. Next time you come we'll dig up some plants you can bring down for your garden."

So I would be going. There was no way out of it. My eyes filled up and I held my breath until the water caught in the lower lids. Then I looked. There stood Aunt Marie. Beside her was Ma. Between them, a sliver of light from the morning sun.

BACK HOME IN A BLUR. Ma in the kitchen, clipping coupons. Pa in his favorite chair, newspaper crackling. Then back in school. I found it hard to concentrate, hard to be where I was. The forest followed me with the strong smell of the cedar wand I kept in my desk. When I closed my math book, the sound was Aunt Marie's breath. In religion class, the spirits hovered and whispered during prayers, and all through science, I heard the call of the sturgeon, blocked by a dam from their ancestral waters. I went through the days as though cloaked in a drift of fog and when the last bell rang, I was the first to leave, slipping out the back door of the classroom before the others had even closed their books. I laid awake most nights, getting more and more anxious as I wondered about Marie, strategized ways I'd get back to the reservation, made my plans.

Then in the third week of school during religion class,

the voices reading aloud turned into the hum of bees. On top of that I thought I heard Marie humming her song. The sound was faint, but my sense of her was as clear as if she were standing beside me. She glowed with irresistible love. I let myself be swallowed by her warmth and my body dissolved into a blissful peace. Then something shook me from the inside out and my hands wouldn't lay still. I felt a sudden dread. Where did she go? Right then, I knew my fate was tied to Aunt Marie's and it didn't look good. Pa used to say that bad things happen in threes, so I started counting.

I looked up. Vickie Vitello sat in front of me, her black fluffy pigtails bouncing as though they were attached with springs. Then I saw they weren't pigtails at all, but weasels, their bodies twisting in frantic lunges, trying to detach from her head. I leaned forward on my desk and kept staring, even after Sister Ambrose told us to go to page 87 and I could hear Vickie Vitello begin to read from the psalms, her voice a lullaby from far away. The weasels bounced in time, soothed by the pretty words, and I sat back in my chair, watching the back of my hands on the desktop as their faint veins became the blue river where the sturgeon used to spawn. From a great distance, someone called my name, but I didn't answer. Instead, I watched as a tiny, distant Marie ran free alongside the river in my hand, hair flying in a silver cloud behind her head.

A movement toward me, like heavy wind, and the flat side of a ruler landed across my knuckles. Instinctively, my hands shot up to my forehead and that's how the water spilled out. I saw Sister Ambrose then, as though we were both underwater in the blue river, all the school desks turned to boulders. She pulled me up by the ear and led me out of the room, the waters whirling around us as we walked. I felt my voice turn into a hollow walnut and drop deep into my belly, and the world took on an underwater silence that made everything slow and spongy.

Sister Ambrose pulled me toward a wooden chair outside the principal's office. I sat there, still underwater, as the two nuns stood over me. Words swam from their mouths and burrowed into the mud, leaving only the urgent, curved tail of their question marks waving like seaweed. I opened my mouth to answer, but only a gurgle came out. The walnut shell that held my voice lay buried in the mud, so I just sat in the chair, my breath turning to bubbles, wishing I could swim.

The bell rang. The two nuns hesitated for a moment, conferred, then let me go.

I RAN MOST OF THE WAY HOME, glad for the wind in my face, and came in through the alley to the backyard, passed the garage with Pa's tomato plants edging it, passed the small strawberry patch that Ma planted in the empty lot next door, passed the old apple tree, limbs heavy with ripening fruit.

I passed through the back porch with Pa's rubber boots and the shelf of old baskets; through the kitchen with its faded linoleum and ancient stove. On the dining room table sat a small green bowl filled with Ma's coupons. Beneath it, a note:

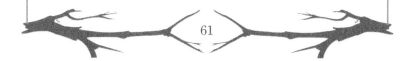

Charlotte,
I went to Belle's to help with the babies. Pa has a union
meeting and won't be home until late. There's leftover cas-
serole. Clean up good, the ants are back.
Love, Ma

Without Ma in it, the silent house felt somber. From
the dining room wall, the faces looked out at me from their
fancy frames: Pa's father, Grandpa Breton, eyes iced over
and far away. Pa told me he left home at 17, crossed half
the country by mule and never looked back. Next to him
was Pa's mother, Grandma Breton, soft and blurry as a
dream, black hair piled atop her head. All I knew about her
was what Pa said: she was an angel, deserved better than
what she got.

I went to the attic door next to the kitchen and up the
linoleum stairs to my room. It used to belong to Belle, who
stuffed it with things that made it feel cozy. Next to that
memory, it felt a little barren. There was the unfinished
plank floor; an oval rug that Ma had braided out of old rags
and outgrown clothes; the rough pine desk that Pa built for
me, its surface covered with dried leaves that I had collected in the fall; and the oak dresser with its rounded
drawers and slender, curved legs that Belle had left behind,
my Grandma Sarah's buttoned up china doll sitting stiff on
its surface. Over the doll's head, Ma had hung a portrait of
Jesus, fire circling his open heart, blood dripping from the
wounds in his palms, eyes dissolving into heaven.

I sat on the bed. In the dim quiet, I sensed a presence
and knew it was Marie. She felt different than she had at

school. There she had been bright, otherworldly, like a visit from the Blessed Mother, and it felt like a dream. But here, she felt ordinary, no different than if she had been at her counter pouring water for tea. The sense of her simply standing there was so strange and real, it filled me with dread.

"I think you should go now," I whispered to the dresser. Then I went downstairs to heat up my dinner.

THE PHONE CALL CAME the next morning, but by the time Ma told me, I already knew Marie was gone. I'd seen it coming from the day she gave up her medicine. When she slipped that vial under Frank's hand, the whole thing was set in motion like a rock tumbling down the mountainside, and I didn't stop it. What child wouldn't have wondered and worried and blamed herself? I knew, and I didn't tell Ma or Grandpa or Belle. Kept the whole thing to myself. And what about the other signs: the vision at school, feeling her by the dresser? She hadn't passed completely over, and what did I do? I asked her to leave.

The guilt and regret sealed me tight on the outside, but inside it splayed me open, and that was all that mattered to them spirits. From that day forward they moved in and out freely, as though my body had a swinging door.

6

THE MOON TOOK MY FINGER

Charlotte

LIFE DOESN'T STOP just because someone dies, and after that day at the apple tree, when Marie came back in the form of a hum, my days blurred into the light and shadow in St. Francis woods where I spent nearly all of my free time. The order of nuns was shrinking, and as I moved from grammar school to high school, I watched from a safe distance as the younger nuns — most already middle-aged — got transferred out one at a time to vacant teaching assignments in other parts of the city. No one came to replace them. By the time I was in my mid-teens, most of the sisters left behind were elderly and never came to the woods.

The first time I saw anyone there was at least a year after Aunt Marie died. I was discovered by the youngest nun, a soft-spoken, girlish woman named Sister Claire who had come to prepare the long-neglected graveyard for the first in a wave of funerals as the older nuns took their leave. She was as shy as I was, so I felt comfortable with her and helped rake and trim in silent companionship. I offered to take care of the new plantings in the cement urns that marked the corners of the graveyard, and did so from then on, watering the ferns in summer, filling in with marigolds in the fall, and keeping the area around the grotto raked so she could take that off her list of chores. She was grateful, as she had to do most of the outdoor work by herself, what with the budget so tight and the other sisters so frail, and she smiled and waved from the back garden whenever she saw me on the path that went into the trees.

I made it my business to accompany the newly released spirits of the nuns after their elderly shells were put into the ground, doing for them what I hadn't done for Marie. I suppose I was looking for atonement. With my gentle encouragement and the steady hum of Marie's song, the new ones passed quickly to the other side, nourished enough by life to be willing to let it go. But not Gustafie. Though I had been with her for so many years, still she wandered there. I was afraid she would linger in those woods forever, long after I had gone myself.

I had always followed Ma's instructions and went to the woods only in the daylight, even though I would have liked to have gone in the evenings, since I'd learned to find comfort in the darkness. I took to climbing onto the eaves outside my window near the apple tree after Ma and Pa had gone to bed. From my perch there, I could hear the hoot of owls and watch the moon do its turning, sometimes shining through the tree branches to make moving tattoos on my arms from shadow and light. Even in the winter I'd go out, as long as the roof was free of ice. I'd bring the quilt from my bed to bundle against the cold.

But then one especially cold night after I had gone to sleep, a blue moon laid its light on my cheek and called to me like a spirit. It was long after midnight and they were asleep, so I had to be careful on the steps from my attic room. I knew where the squeaks were, which boards to avoid. I closed the back screen door in the slowest increments, and then I was free. The light from that moon did something to my blood. I felt it crackling in me while I walked through the dark city streets alone, playing with the hole in the fingertip of my glove. The moon lit the streets in the colors of a dream.

When I got to the woods, I didn't take the path to the graveyard. Instead, I went into the pines. I sat on a rotting log where the moonlight could pool on my face and soaked it up like a thirsty plant. Tears came and they got cold so fast, dripping from my chin — so cold I thought they'd make icicles. The wind gathered powder from little patches of snow, swirled it around me and through the tree limbs. I lay back on the log and watched the treetops dance, lit by moonlight, patterns from the pine branches falling over me like a blanket. Then I felt Gustafie there, tugging. She had never tugged on me before.

The wind stopped abruptly. I felt hypnotized, the air suddenly still. My mind melted into the sky. As if on their own, my arms flung to the ground and my back arched, chest reaching for the moon. Gustafie hovered right over me — I could feel the density of her, almost suffocating. Then the moonlight poured right through her and into my chest, filling it like a vase, and I saw what she needed me to see and felt what she needed me to feel: her father sick from a war injury and the journey across the sea; her mother scrubbing the floors at the grocer to buy food; she on the steps of the convent, with no English and an obscure dialect of German no one could understand. They took her in and wouldn't let her mother visit. That was policy, but she didn't know. Alone with her language and her grief, she made herself sick and never found her way. All she needed was for someone to see her, someone to feel her. Then the moonlight flowed through my veins — rivers and streams of moonlight — and I was a forest, made of light, cradling a luminous graveyard where the soul of Gustafie finally let go and dissolved into the sky.

Things went black. When I woke up, the moon had moved in an arc away from the log and my body was vibrating with cold. My right hand rested in a cradle of snow and I couldn't feel my fingers, just a strange thickness and electric pinging. I stood, shivering. How could I walk with all of this shaking inside? But somehow I did with the help of a tree branch that I used as a cane, resting my numb hand on its end. Later, I discovered it had made an inch-long gash in my palm, but I didn't feel it then. My black glove swallowed the blood so I couldn't see.

I got home just before dawn. Thankfully the house was still dark. I opened the screen door as slow as I could, but my hands had no sensitivity, and my limbs still vibrated with cold. The door let out a squeal and I couldn't keep it from banging a little once I got inside. I inched my way across the kitchen toward the attic door, watching my feet so I wouldn't hit a chair leg.

When I got near the kitchen door, I saw the hem of Ma's cotton nightgown against her sturdy calves. A flash of her face, washed with surprise and fright, and then her arms were supporting me, silently moving me toward the attic door. Now we were in it together, and we had to do it without waking Pa. Ma left me leaning against the wall for a minute while she tiptoed back and closed her bedroom door. Then we worked our way up the steps in painful slowness, until finally I was sitting on the edge of my bed, bones chattering, as Ma went about the work of thawing me out. Her face was hard with questions and worry.

"Where did you go?" she whispered.

"To the woods."

"In the middle of the night?"

"It was bright as day. I swear I've never done it before. It was the moon."

I was surprised when Ma's face softened. She looked at me with a curious recognition. Then fear shadowed her eyes and she hardened again.

"You have to be more careful. You could have woken your Pa. And you nearly lost your fingers."

Really, it's a miracle I had any hands left at all, given what they looked like when Ma pulled off my gloves. The gash had stopped bleeding by then, but my fingers looked otherworldly, like they belonged on a corpse. She saved all of them except the one that had poked through the hole and rested naked in the snow. That one withered into a wrinkled, purple bruise, and it had to be removed just above the second knuckle. By the time Pa came home from work, Ma had thought of a story to use. She told Pa I'd worked too long clearing the snow from in front of the cellar, even though it was she who had done the shoveling. Pa just said, "How many times do I have to tell you? Two layers of mitts," and he left it at that.

AFTER THAT NIGHT with Gustafie, it was as though the force of gravity didn't apply to me. I was a magnet that turned to the sky and in doing so, lost my footing on the earth. My hands never quite returned to normal. They tingled at the slightest change of temperature, and when I touched something that belonged to someone else, I would get feelings in my gut that weren't mine. To dull the sensations, I took to wearing a pair of ivory dress gloves that Belle had worn to her homecoming dance and had left on the shelf in the front hall closet. When I went to the woods, I wore the gloves plus two pair of mitts, just as Pa said, but not for the reason he thought. My hands knew too much when they were bare, and in the woods, they were picking up more than I could handle.

Though the spirit of Gustafie had left the night the moon took my finger, still there was a residue of all that had happened to the first wave of nuns who had lived there. Beneath that was another residue left from even further back, when people who knew the trees as I knew them had walked and sung there. Sensations and pictures came in through my fingers whenever I touched things, and all through that winter, the gloves and mitts helped me regulate them.

In a certain spot near the meadow, no amount of mitts would help. I discovered it when I came upon an old cedar tree deep in an overgrown part of the woods where I had never gone before. I had Pa's clippers with me. I was using them to trim through underbrush for a foot path, and decided to cut a bough of cedar from a low hanging branch to make into wands, as Marie had taught me. The wood was tough, the clippers dull, and it took some effort. When I finished, I leaned against the trunk to rest.

As soon as my back touched the bark, it was as though I had stepped into another time. My head went light and I sat on the ground, eyes blurred, head pounding. Then not with the eyes I saw things. More I sensed them, felt them, and snatches came clear in my vision like they were really there. I don't know when all these things happened — just that they did.

I saw that this had been part of a summer camp for a band of people who had hunted in the area for hundreds of years — maybe even thousands. One year when the weather was gentle, they came late to the camp. In that time, others had come from far away, and when the tribe returned, this corner of the camp, which they normally used for ceremony, was occupied with two families of settlers, just beginning to down the trees and build homes.

I saw the men with their axes, the children playing near a canvas tent, a string of laundry. Then I saw the men with rifles, shouts, confusion, the sky thick with fear. A child was trampled by horses, another one shot by mistake, and six men lay bleeding on the grass. Instinctively, my arms reached for the trampled boy, but my hands went right through him. I sat on the ground, sobbing, arms wrapped around my knees, helpless to stop what had already happened, watching his blood form a pool on the grass. The vision faded, but still I heard him moaning.

The woods that had been such a comfort to me now felt sinister. I gathered up Pa's clippers and the cedar I had cut and quickly left for home, head pounding hard as though

the hurt took up the whole sky.

When I came up the back steps, I was surprised to find Belle at the kitchen table sipping coffee with Ma, both of them laughing. She didn't come over as much since she started having babies — Ma usually went there to help. Normally I would have lingered in the warmth of them, but this time I hurried through, wanting just to be alone on my bed.

"Wait Charlotte," Ma said to my back. "Belle has some news."

"I'm going to have another baby," Belle said. "That makes half a dozen." She and Ma laughed. I stood frozen by the kitchen door. I knew if I said anything I would start crying again, and I couldn't let them see. I didn't want to spoil this moment for them.

"Charlotte, what's wrong?" Belle said. I heard her chair scrape and she was coming toward me. How could I explain what I didn't understand myself?

"Just tired," I mumbled. It came out strange, like I was talking inside a tunnel. Before she could reach me, I ran up the attic stairs and curled myself into a ball on the bed, pretending to sleep, but I couldn't stop their footsteps on the staircase. I didn't realize I was still clutching the cedar until I felt Ma take it from my hand and put it on the floor near the dresser.

"What happened?" she said. I kept my eyes closed, trying to find words, but none came. Ma put her hand on my forehead.

"Is she warm?" I heard Belle say.

"You can get her some tea," Ma said, and I heard Belle's heels tap their way back down the stairs.

"Something happened in the woods," Ma said when the stairwell was quiet.

"It wasn't from now," I said, knowing it wouldn't make any sense. A sob tried to escape, but I choked it down.

Ma covered me with the blankets. "Stay away from the woods for a few days. Rest yourself."

I felt a wave of gratitude for her, so strong it almost felt painful. I took her hand and gave it a squeeze, then kissed it.

Ma touched my hair. "You can tell me if you want."

I squeezed her hand again. I would have told her everything then, but before I could speak I heard Belle on the staircase, the spoon rattling against the saucer. Ma got the tea from her and left it next to my bed.

"She's not feeling well," I heard her say to Belle. "She's glad for your baby."

7

WOMB IN THE SKY

Lata

THE DAY THAT UNCLE JESSE finished stripping the banister in the front hallway and started on the stairs themselves, Aunt Charlotte claimed the sunroom, a small room off the hallway that Uncle Jesse hadn't gotten to yet. The room was a bit like a porch jutting out into the backyard and it had its own roof so it was a little hotter than the rest of the house, though the stone floor gave it a pleasing coolness underfoot. The wall adjoining the dining room held a fireplace with an embossed metal face, and Aunt Charlotte had put a vase of flowers where the fire would normally be. Ancient faded wallpaper covered the walls and the slate blue paint was easy to peel off the woodwork around the large bay window that looked out at the oak tree. I worked at the chips with my fingernail, revealing old layers of yellow and dusty pink.

Meanwhile, Aunt Charlotte brought in a ratty, oversized chair with scratchy green upholstery. Behind the chair she placed the Victorian floor lamp we'd found at the garage sale. She covered the cord with electrical tape to be safe, but you had to turn it on with just the right pressure to keep it from flickering and buzzing like a housefly.

On the wall in the sunroom, over dank wallpaper the color of tea, Aunt Charlotte hung pictures of her ancestors, which I later realized were my ancestors, too: plain, flat, serious faces framed with hair shiny and black as raven's wings, dressed in stiff clothing that looked like it pinched. In one photo, a group of them sat on rickety wooden chairs in a muddy clearing outside a tiny farmhouse. One of the men held a drum in his lap. They had dragged an upright piano out of the house for the photo and a solid-looking man with chiseled features leaned against it.

This man, Aunt Charlotte told me, was my Great Grandpa Abe, a French/Mascoutin fisherman who died before I was born. The woman beside him was his wife, my Great Grandma Sarah, a mixed-blood Menominee who Charlotte never met. Beside this photo she hung a portrait, small and murky, of a woman with a broad face and squinting black eyes. This woman, she told me, was my Aunt Marie, Grandma Emmie's sister. As a child, Aunt Charlotte had stayed a few days with Aunt Marie at the tiny farmhouse in the picture.

When Aunt Charlotte was done hanging the pictures, she sat in the green armchair and pulled her legs up under her like a girl. She seemed charged, somehow, and her hands made slight flitting movements like little birds. Though I couldn't have said it then, I knew that the photos were an invitation to the ghosts from an old tragedy. I sat at her feet and could feel those ghosts scrambling over the windowsills into the house, tracking mud and rose petals from the garden.

FOR THE REST OF THE SUMMER, Aunt Charlotte lived in the sunroom and entered the rest of the house only in the morning to wash up and boil water for tea. She kept a bowl of fruit next to her chair and stopped eating dinner with me and Uncle Jesse. She was fasting, she said, because she needed answers. Besides, she told Uncle Jesse when he protested, fruit was plenty in the heat. She took to sleeping outside in a hammock that she strung between the house and a gnarled oak tree outside the sunroom window. She kept the window open and would move from sunroom to garden as it suited her. Uncle Jesse said it was dangerous to do this in the city, and pleaded with her to come inside at night, but Aunt Charlotte wouldn't be swayed. When I told Aunt Charlotte I wanted to sleep outside with her, she agreed to allow it as long as I came down after Uncle Jesse had gone to sleep and got up before he left for work.

Those summer nights, Aunt Charlotte would sometimes walk restlessly in the garden lit only by the faint light from the Victorian lamp fluttering through the sunroom window. She looked feral in the darkness, like an animal that had sprung from the woods, born to wolves and raised on the eggs of wild birds. Once I saw a deep shadow shaped like a bear following her. It frightened me.

We slept together in the hammock rolled in a white cotton sheet. I never slept so well as I did under the night sky with Aunt Charlotte's warm, rhythmic breath stroking my neck, the rise and fall of her chest against my back. I would try to match her breathing until our chests rose and fell in unison and we drew in the same warm air. We were twins, snug in a womb suspended in the sky. We would wake early with the sun, covered in dew, and tell each other our dreams.

When I was with Aunt Charlotte, dreams were more real than gravity. Those early mornings in the hammock, we could take our time, tell every detail, until the dreams took on a physical quality, as though we were fingering bits of seashell and shiny stones picked up from the beach. Sometimes Aunt Charlotte would begin to tell her dream and I would be certain that I had dreamed the same thing. Then we would tell it together, each filling in what the other had forgotten.

AFTER A FEW WEEKS, Aunt Charlotte's fruit fast began to show in her body. Her arms lost their roundness and seemed woody, like tree branches barely covered with skin. Her movements took on a deliberate quality, as though it took conscious effort to lift her arm or turn her head. As her body slowed, so did her activity. We stopped taking cuttings from the plants to make more, and gradually, she stopped tending the garden altogether. It quickly grew into a wild tangle of stems, leaves and blossoms, more field than yard.

She took to sitting on the ground amongst the plants for hours at a time, humming softly as she watched the leaves dance, listening to the bees and crickets, examining the flowers in every stage of growth — from tiny bump, to bud, to blossom, to the structure left when the petals fell. I often sat with her, though the insect life grew denser as the plants thickened and I couldn't bear to have them crawling over my legs, so I'd sometimes bring a sheet from

inside and wrap myself in it. I offered to share it with Aunt Charlotte, but the bugs never bothered her. They crawled over her as though she were a fallen log. The longer we sat together humming her little melody in that field of flowers and insects, the more vivid each plant became, until they took on a sense of being that felt no different than if a person were sitting there. In time, the bugs did the same, and I found myself letting the sheet drop away as I leaned elbows into the earth to examine more closely the wing of a fly or the knees of a grasshopper.

One hot afternoon as we sat amongst the plants, I noticed that some in the full sun looked weakened, their leaves turning brown. I reached for the empty watering can. Aunt Charlotte put her hand on my arm.

"It's okay, Lata. We can't baby them forever," she said. "We did our best to find them their places. It's time for the plants to survive on their own."

It bothered me not to water the plants, but at the same time, something told me she was right.

ALL SUMMER LONG, we didn't see much of Uncle Jesse. He spent long hours at the construction site, finishing up as many new houses as possible while the weather was good, and when he did have time at home, he worked at stripping the floors and then covering them with thin coats of varnish. Normally he left the house at eight, so if I got up by six, it was in plenty of time to leave the hammock. But one morning, he was up at dawn, and I woke in the hammock beside Aunt Charlotte to find him staring at us, bewildered. When he saw that I was awake, he turned and

made his way through the tangle of plants, shoulders hunched, and got into his van. As he backed out of the drive, the exhaust drifted to the hammock, settling in the grass, and that smell was Jesse's loneliness.

A spell had been broken and so we didn't linger like we usually did. Instead, Aunt Charlotte slid from the hammock, landing lightly on the dry earth below. She had a way of placing her feet as though every step were alive with feeling and I tried to copy her grace, but I was too short and landed with a thud. She went inside the house and I could hear water running in the kitchen. I wasn't ready to go in yet, so I swung with my belly against the hammock, dragging my toes over the dusty earth. I loved going barefoot. Aunt Charlotte said it was a shame to imprison our feet in shoes when the ground was so inviting — and I agreed.

I heard a car drive up and park in front. A man with slicked back hair emerged from a white chevy, wearing a pressed shirt with a navy blue tie. At first he just stood there on the sidewalk examining the house and making tick marks on the clipboard he held in the crook of his arm. Then he strode up the path and swung open the gate as though he owned the place, wiggling a ballpoint pen between his fingers like a baton.

"You're going to break that hammock, little lady," the man said to me.

"No I won't." I pulled back on the hammock and swung again, lifting my feet so they wouldn't slow the momentum.

"Shouldn't pull on the middle like that. Puts too much

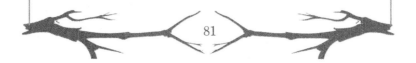

81

stress in one spot. It's not built for what you're doing."

"Aunt Charlotte doesn't mind."

"Oh she doesn't, does she."

I could hear the rope creaking against the hook in the tree and stopped the swing with my feet, just in case he was right. He walked over to the house and squatted beside the window well that went to the basement, peering down as though he'd lost something.

"What're you looking for?"

"Seems I found it. Cracks in the foundation." He stood up, looking pleased with himself, and put his palm on the trunk of the old oak. "This tree has to go. Way too close to the house. Should have come out years ago."

"That tree's more than 200 years old," I heard Aunt Charlotte say. She had come out of the kitchen and was standing in the back door, still in her white cotton nightgown, a cup of tea in her hand.

"A menace," he said absently. "Trees should never be planted near houses." He was scratching a note on his clipboard.

"It was here long before the house," Aunt Charlotte said.

"Maybe they shouldn't put houses near trees," I said, trying to be helpful. I looked up into the wide canopy of the oak. The morning sun soaked into the leaves so completely, they looked as though they were made of light.

"Like she says, you have it backwards, sir," Aunt Charlotte said. She was walking toward us now with a strange, powerful gait, like a lion about to pounce. "I assume you're from the insurance company? Jesse said you'd be coming."

The man nodded. "Anthony Jarvis, Statewide Insurance." He reached out his hand, but Aunt Charlotte didn't take it. Instead, she put her palm on my shoulder. There was a tremble in it that wasn't fear — something strong that I sensed could hurt him if he got too close.

"You'll get good money for that oak," he said, going back to his clipboard. "Will help you pay for the repairs on the foundation. The rest of the work on the house looks good, but we can't insure it until this is done."

"Tree is more important than the house."

The man looked up at Aunt Charlotte. He seemed unnerved by her, as though it were wrong to value a living tree over something made from dead ones.

"Sorry to disturb you so early," he said. "I'll just take a walk around the house to check a few more things, and then be on my way."

THAT EVENING, Uncle Jesse got home particularly late, so Aunt Charlotte got dinner for me and then we sat in the sunroom curled together in the green armchair, paging through a library book about the medicinal uses of tree bark. The Victorian lamp was unplugged and stood in a shadow by the window. When the darkness dimmed the page too much to comfortably see the pictures, I got up to plug in the lamp, but Aunt Charlotte stopped me.

"No more electricity, Lata," she said. "From now on, we can only use candles." She lit a white taper on the table beside the chair.

"How will we see the pictures?" I asked, though once the candle was lit, the glow of the room was so welcoming,

I didn't care much anymore about the book.

"We'll read when it's daylight," she said. "I heard that the government ordered the removal of a tribe from their ancestral home because they found coal in the mountain. How can we use electricity when that's how they get it?" Her face had a pained expression, as though they had taken her own home to get the coal.

She sat back down in the green armchair and I sat beside her, my legs stretched over her lap. I could feel her heart beating hard, like a drum. I looked at the wall in front of us where she had hung the pictures of the ancestors, and imagined myself at the piano where I would start to play a funny, light-hearted song and all the people in their stiff clothes would dance. My fantasy was interrupted by the scrape of Uncle Jesse's boots on the mat. His heavy steps approached the sunroom and he stood in the doorway looking in the candlelight somehow taller and more grim than usual.

"Insurance man came," Aunt Charlotte said.

"I already talked to him."

"Well then you know they're not taking the tree," Aunt Charlotte said, and before he could answer, she brushed past him and out the back door. Uncle Jesse twisted around to watch her, and I thought he might follow, but then the screen door banged shut and he turned back to me.

"Come on, Lata, it's bed time." I slid from the armchair and went to him. He smelled of something smoky, like after a campfire. He took my hand and led me up the stairs.

As I changed into my pajamas, he stood at the bedroom window looking into the backyard, where I knew Aunt

Charlotte was likely sitting amongst the plants in the light of the moon. I slipped into bed and closed my eyes immediately, pretending to sleep. I felt his eyes on me as he walked to the side of the bed and settled the sheet around my shoulders. I wanted him to leave but instead he sat on the wide ledge of the window, looking out over the part of the garden where Aunt Charlotte's hammock swung.

He stayed there for what seemed like hours, and after a while I was exhausted by how his presence seemed to draw air from the room. With my thoughts I tried to push him into his own room so I could go to Aunt Charlotte in the hammock but he just kept sitting there, and my frustration brought tears. I tried to muffle them in the pillow but that only made me gasp for air. I felt the bed sink and Uncle Jesse was sitting beside me, his big hand trembling as he stroked my hair. I could feel his fear and sadness. This made me cry harder because I had to cry for both of us. Finally I fell asleep to his gentle, awkward touch.

THAT NIGHT, I DREAMED I was at the farm in Aunt Charlotte's photograph, playing the piano for the relatives as they danced. A man sat beside me beating a drum that was painted with rings of red and yellow. Aunt Charlotte was there too, the worn leather tobacco pouch strung around her neck. She was dancing and laughing. I had never seen her so vibrant. Then I heard a siren and knew the police were coming to arrest us because there was coal under the house and they wanted to get it. Everyone scattered into the woods and the police went after them, so I ran into the farmhouse and hid in a closet.

I stayed there for a long time. I could hear banging, loud voices, the sound of machinery — they were digging for the coal. I was hungry and frightened and thought I might die there. Then it got quiet. I heard a voice outside the door and knew that it was Aunt Marie.

"Poor little girl," she said. "It's time to come out now. Don't be afraid. I have a gift for you."

I opened the closet door. The room was empty. Outside the window, I could see a large group of people. Uncle Jesse was there and so were the police. They were having a picnic. There were hotdogs on the grill and big plates of brownies.

"Go on, now," the voice said kindly. "Get yourself something to eat."

I stepped quietly down the steps, right past two police officers, but they just kept eating their brownies. I went to get a hot dog from the grill and noticed Uncle Jesse's paint chips fluttering over the coals. I couldn't read their names except for Sienna Suede, the color he had chosen for the front hallway. I saw then that the fire was built from the banister that Uncle Jesse had just refinished. The leather pouch that Aunt Charlotte had been wearing earlier in the dream was nudged right under that wood.

I flicked up the edge of the grill and grabbed for it, fingers stinging from the heat. It was scorched black on one side but still intact. I wanted to look closer but heard someone behind me, so I slipped it into my pocket just as Uncle Jesse put his hand on my shoulder. I was afraid he had seen the pouch and would take it away from me, but he just offered me a hot dog and patted me on the head.

I woke up, then, because Uncle Jesse's hand really was

on my shoulder and he really was patting my head. At first, the bedroom looked unfamiliar. I was so used to waking up under the sky next to Aunt Charlotte, and my dream had been so vivid that I thought I could be back in the farmhouse. I wanted to go back to sleep and finish the dream, but Uncle Jesse was pulling me up by the hands, calling me lazy bones.

When I got to the kitchen, Aunt Charlotte was not there and the kettle for her tea was not on the burner. Uncle Jesse had poured me a glass of orange juice and was putting bread in the toaster. I started toward the sunroom, but he stopped me.

"Sit down and drink your juice," he said, and he steered me by the shoulders back to the kitchen table. I squirmed, but he was firm.

"I want to get Aunt Charlotte," I said. "I'll be right back."

Uncle Jesse didn't answer. There was something alarming about his silence and I knew then that Aunt Charlotte wasn't in the house.

"Where is she?" I demanded. I could feel the heat rise in my cheeks.

Uncle Jesse knelt beside me and put his hand on my knee. "Calm down," he said. "She just had to do some shopping. She'll be back by lunchtime."

"Aunt Charlotte doesn't like to shop," I said, because I thought he might be lying.

"But she'll do it when someone is about to turn eight." He patted my knee. "Okay now?"

I nodded, but it wasn't okay.

I stayed alert and a little frightened until just after noon

when I found Aunt Charlotte back in her sunroom, sitting in the green armchair, eating a plum. I sat next to her on the chair and laid my head against her shoulder. She put her arm around me in the easy, comfortable way she had and offered me a bite of the plum. Its sweet, heady juice dripped down my chin and landed in a thick line on her forearm. She wiped it up with her thumb and put it to my lips. I licked off the juice, now flavored with the faint taste of her skin — a dim, subtle flavor a bit like vanilla bean that existed only there. I have never tasted it since. We were facing the wall with the pictures of the ancestors.

"I dreamed about them last night," I said, absently pointing toward the pictures.

Aunt Charlotte sat up straighter and turned toward me. "What happened?" she said with an urgency that surprised me.

Looking at the photos on the wall, the dream came back in vivid detail and I told her everything, enjoying the intensity of her attention. "There would have been more," I said, still looking at the photos. "But Uncle Jesse woke me up."

I turned toward Aunt Charlotte. Her face was flushed and her eyes looked unnaturally bright. "This is an important dream," she said. "Aunt Marie came to you. Are you sure it was Aunt Marie? Did you see her?"

"I didn't see her, but I knew it was her voice."

"Maybe you'll finish the dream tonight. You'll have to try." She spoke with an urgency that troubled me.

8

CALLED BACK BY THE SPIRITS

Charlotte

I DIDN'T GO BACK to the woods for what felt like a long time. It had become the site of a relentless massacre — one that was still happening as far as I was concerned, even as life continued in its ordinary way. The longer I stayed away, the more my hands calmed down, but still I wore Belle's old prom gloves — even indoors — to keep from getting a jolt. People got used to them in a hurry, and as a bonus, no one commented on the missing tip of my finger.

It was a bitterly cold winter, with icicles long as spears hanging from the garage and I spent more time indoors than ever in my life. From this distance, the woods took on a dreamlike quality, as though they had escaped their iron fence and now floated above the city like a storm cloud. I felt the pressure of that cloud most when I was alone, so for the first time in my life, I sought out the company of others.

On school nights, instead of going upstairs to my bedroom, where even with the space heater on high I could see my breath, I took to doing my homework at the dining room table while Pa read the newspaper in the adjoining living room, stretched out in his favorite chair. I was surprised by how companionable it felt: Pa in his baggy dungarees, socked feet up on the vinyl hassock, reading glasses perched on the tip of his nose. Ma would sometimes sit with me to do her crossword puzzle, but more often she'd settle into a corner of the couch and click her black rosary beads, the murmur of prayer under her breath.

On Sundays, I started going to church with her. She liked to go to the 7am Mass — too early for all the big families with their squirming children. Pa never came with us. He didn't like the Catholics much, though I never found out why, and I only ever went with Ma if I really wanted to. Pa said people had a right to their own beliefs and it was up to me to decide. Even though it wasn't in Ma's nature to push anything, she seemed to like it when I came.

Ma liked to sit near the statue of Mary, who rose above a sea of votive candles flickering in their burgundy glasses. Before Mass started, we always stood at the statue, and Ma would watch intently as I lit a candle for Aunt Marie, but once seated in the pew, she hardly noticed me, what with how deep inside herself she'd get as she fingered her rosary all through the service. Meanwhile, I would stare at the enormous golden Jesus hanging on a cross over the altar so I wouldn't miss the moment when his crown of thorns sent out shimmers of light — which it did every time the heater's fan blew hard against the brass lamps that hung on chains from the ceiling.

I would have liked to have gone on this way clear until summer, snug and peaceful with Ma and Pa, but then Pa took the lead in organizing a strike at Hoover Glass where he worked as a glass cutter, and on the night of Ash Wednesday, when Ma and I came back from church with fore-heads still smudged grey, I found the dining room table was no longer mine. Now it belonged to the union men, who left their claim on Ma's good tablecloth in the form of violet smears from their carbon paper and rust-colored rings from their coffee mugs. Cigar ashes and shiny bits of cellophane littered the rug.

Pa didn't want the meetings disturbed, so from that night on, if I didn't go to my room right after dinner, I wasn't allowed to go through the kitchen door to get there. I still didn't want to be alone, so night after night, Ma and I stayed in the kitchen together. The noise from the next room — not to mention the stink of cigars — wasn't conducive to our usual activities, so we made applesauce and sweet breads until we used up all the apples stored in the cellar. Then we organized the pantry, washed all the spice jars, oiled all the cast iron pots. Still, the men kept coming.

Without the woods to balance it, all of that concentrated doing with Ma brought me back to earth in a way I wasn't used to. My attention went to the edges of things, how every pot in the sink was powerfully distinct and separate from the others. A plainness to it all, this world where things were what they seemed to be. From this vantage point, I saw myself as others might see me: strange, withdrawn, eyes looking off at nothing. I felt shame rise. No wonder I had no friends. In the solid world, I was defective. My thoughts took on a harshness I wasn't used to, a violence that got fed by the dense talk of the union men, who were sure that treachery was real.

In the routine of those nights in the kitchen, the dining

room belching cigar smoke, dark cold pressing through the window, I thought I might be stuck forever in this solid, merciless world. A sadness came over me. Maybe my soul had left for good, suffocated by the density of it all. But then one night in the heavy rock of sleep that had become so familiar, something burrowed through from the other side. It started with a steady hum that gradually shifted into a deafening sound — the thunder of a fallen tree. I saw the cedar tree at Aunt Marie's — or was it the one at St. Francis woods? Out of nowhere, heart pounding, I sat up in bed as though in an emergency. The spirits couldn't wait any longer. I was being called back from my solid, padded life — back to the woods, where I went early the next morning.

I LEFT THE HOUSE BEFORE DAWN, unable to wait any longer. Even though the weather had warmed considerably and much of the snow had melted, the early morning air had a bite to it. In my rush to get to the woods, I had forgotten both hat and mitts, so by the time I reached the entrance gate, my fingers were already tingling in the thin cotton felt of Belle's prom gloves.

The convent shone dim yellow light through the upper windows and the Sisters' early morning chants had a velvet quality that followed me down the path leading to the graveyard. There, the crocus bulbs I had planted last fall as a favor to Sister Claire pushed their way up, and at the end of the last row of head stones, a fresh grave was marked and ready to be dug. The grotto looked the same, except for a drift of snow at Mary's feet, protected from the sun by a heavy cover of pine and the embrace of the hill into which it was dug.

I went deeper into the woods, looking for the narrow footpath I had cut that led to the old cedar, but the density of the trees had prevented the sun from reaching all the snow, and the remaining white drifts threw me off, sending me to a number of dead ends. I gave up on my eyes then, as they couldn't do the job, and listened instead to the growing tension in my gut as I moved through underbrush and over patches of ice, feeling my way back further and further into the thickness of the trees until time began to bend — and suddenly the spirits were there, urgent, pushing me through when the way seemed blocked, pulling me over fallen logs and through dense thickets of sumac, then back into the pines until I stumbled over a fallen branch and landed palms down at the far end of a clearing, directly across from the grove of trees ruled by the old cedar. I heard a roar inside, for the clearing was not natural. Some-one had taken a chainsaw to the trees, and their fresh stumps stuck up from the ground like flesh wounds.

The spirits were dense, angry, and pushed their way into me in a rush. I couldn't stop them from using my eyes, my heart. They spun me around, showed me where a driveway had been cut through the iron fence, which had been dismantled for at least 20 feet at the far end of the sister's property. I walked the driveway to the street and read the sign posted there: *Coming soon! Your all new Kroemer Department Store.* The drawing told me all I needed to know: This clearing was only the beginning, meant for the auto repair center. There was still the warehouse, and the store itself would fill up half the block and turn the corner with its large display windows, taking out another huge portion of the woods.

I looked across the wide street to the row of buildings on the other side that stretched back further than I could see. That's when it hit me: all of it had been part of these woods — including the house I lived in. One at a time, the trees were cut, concrete poured, lawns planted, electric wires strung. I thought of Aunt Marie, how she wouldn't let me take the pine cone without saying the good I would do with it, wouldn't let me pick a carrot without giving something back in thanks. Did anyone make their prayers to the forest, make their case for the good this city would do by rising up in its place? Did anyone talk to the people who had lived there first, convince them of the pressing need for the giant dry cleaner and the drug store and the factory that made foam rubber? The spirits made it be known: no one had asked — they had just taken. And the taking hadn't stopped.

By then, the sun had risen higher, its light turning to glare on the bus that belched fumes at the corner as it waited for the light to change. For so long, when I had gone to the woods, it was as though entering the gate brought me into a different world, unaffected by the solid one that held cars and shops, schools and union men. But now I saw with stark clarity that the woods only existed because of a delicate balance of factors easily disrupted by the dwindling budget of the Order of the Sisters of Saint Francis, easily crushed by the density and appetite of the newer world that pressed up against it. Now that the fence was torn away, the dense world spilled in like a cancer, ready to eat up what little remained of the forest.

Something rose up inside me — a heat unfamiliar that might not have been mine, seeing as those spirits were clamoring inside. This had to stop. And I had to stop it.

I GOT THROUGH THE SCHOOL DAY in a blur, my mind busy with planning and worry. All the while, I was aware that the school itself came to be in the same way as the department store, and a bitter aversion grew in me. How could I be there at all, participating in such destruction? My heart was a magnet for all those spirits who had been dismissed and belittled by the arrogant knowing of those who ordered the trees cut, the earth paved over, the children put into uniforms and seated in rows at little desks. *I don't have to sit here, just because they want me to. I can get up and leave right now.* But no, I had to be smart about it. For years, I had cultivated a way of moving through the world that rendered me invisible. Now I would put that skill to good use.

When the last bell rang, I was the first out the door and went immediately to the woods. I decided to go a different way this time, down the sidewalk that bordered the spot where the fence had been dismantled. Even from a distance, I could see that the area was buzzing with activity. A truck sat in the new driveway, its cab blocking the sidewalk. A pickup waited on the roadside, engine running, along with a shiny black car. Two men in suits stood beside the truck, conferring with a man in a white hard hat and another in dungarees, who I recognized as one of the union men who had come to see Pa a few times last fall when he first started talking about a strike. A machine roared somewhere in the woods.

From the vantage point of the sidewalk, it was all over. Contracts had been signed and the work had begun in earnest. I was just a strange girl, inept in this world. What did those spirits expect me to do? I turned around, heavy with grief, and headed home.

THAT NIGHT, the union meeting went on longer than ever. Ma and I stayed at the kitchen table playing Canasta until almost midnight waiting for the men to finish, our eyes dry and red from the cigar smoke seeping under the door. By then, our time in the kitchen had lost any semblance of usefulness. We were just going through the motions to distract ourselves from the slow movement of the clock. It occurred to me for the first time that no one had ever asked us if we minded being locked away in the kitchen for endless weeks with the rancid smell of cheap cigar smoke. Finally, we heard them push the chairs out and rustle into their coats.

As soon as the voices faded, Ma opened the kitchen door. The dining room was grey with smoke and I could taste the cigars all the way down my throat. I watched the last of the men file through the front door and recognized one of them as the man I had seen at the building site earlier. He said something to Pa as he stepped onto the porch. Then I heard Pa say, "That's right, Eddie. It's in the can. No stoppin' us now."

We had the table almost cleared by the time Pa came

back in. Normally he walked with the bent posture of an old man, but that night he stood straight and vigorous, as though he were 20 years younger. Even his clothes looked different, though he was wearing the same red plaid shirt as he always did, and the same brown suspenders holding up the same pair of dungarees.

"Well, Mommy, we're going to do it," Pa said. "On Monday when the whistle blows, them bosses are in for a big surprise."

"And you're sure they don't know it's you behind it?"

"Seems they don't know nothing yet. We kept a damn good secret."

"Let's hope so," Ma said as she gathered the last of the empty coffee cups and ash-covered saucers onto a tray.

"Charlotte, honey, take this to the kitchen for me, then get yourself up to bed."

"I know it's gone late," Pa said with an odd buoyancy. "Couldn't be helped."

I took the tray from Ma and put it on the kitchen counter.

"You did what you had to do," I heard Ma say, her voice a little pinched. "Just don't go getting yourself hurt."

"It'll be all right — them union boys are watching out for me. We're holding out for a five-cent raise now that we got the Kroemer contract to pressure them with. Them Kroemer brothers are putting up new stores all over the city, and we're doing the glass. Hoover don't want to risk losing that one. We got it in the can, Mommy, we got it in the can."

When I came back into the dining room, Pa was putting

his arms around Ma, his face soft and flushed. "Haven't been away from this city for almost twelve years. Once this strike is over and the raise kicks in, I'm going to take my girls some place special." He kissed Ma's forehead, then winked at me. Usually I felt privileged by Pa's wink, but this time I wasn't so sure, given what I'd just heard him say about Kroemer.

"Look how big you're getting," Pa said, as if seeing me for the first time. "Almost as tall as your Ma."

Ma pulled away from him and turned toward me, her face pale and tired. "You still down here? Didn't I say it was bedtime?"

I LAY AWAKE IN BED, wrapped in darkness and the faint smell of cigars. My mind churned out images of the clear-cut end of Saint Francis woods, so dangerously close to the old cedar. Mixed in was the image of Pa's buoyant step when the union men left, the light in his face. He wasn't thinking about the trees. Had he ever been in those woods? Had any of those union men? Probably not. Pa spent most of his time at work — at least as much time as I spent in the woods. I'd never thought before about what he was doing there, what that glass he cut would be used for. And now I saw: display windows. What else was cut and dug and destroyed to make all the shiny things they would put in those windows?

I thought of Aunt Marie scattering her tobacco for each carrot and got out of my warm bed, dragging the quilt with me. In the second drawer of my dresser, I found the to-bacco pouch buried under my sweaters. Since I had long ago run out of tobacco, I had stopped using it. Now I saw what a mistake that was. In the corner by the window was the cedar bough I had cut months ago to make wands. In my fear, I'd left it there, and now it was brittle. I took a handful of the dried cedar needles and stuffed it into the tobacco pouch as best I could. They stuck to my sweater and spilled onto the floor. I pulled tight the drawstring of the tobacco pouch and put the long loop end over my head.

I pulled on coat and gloves, grabbed the cedar bough, and left quietly through the kitchen door, taking a box of matches from the stove as I left. I didn't know exactly what I would do when I got to the woods, but something told me I needed these things that Aunt Marie had given me. I needed her help, and it had been a long time since I had heard her song. I tried to hum it as I walked the empty streets toward St. Francis woods, but it didn't sound right.

The streetlights were still on when I came to the edge of the woods where the iron fence had been removed. I walked through the opening and could smell the cut pine before I could see the discarded limbs of the trees heaped at the driveway's end. Next to them stood a massive rectangle covered in green tarps. I knelt and shone my flashlight underneath. Wood, neatly stacked on pallets — enough to build the frame for the auto repair store, was my guess. Somewhere, another forest had been cut to make those boards. Beside the wood stood a small, makeshift wooden structure with a padlock on its door. Inside, I guessed, were the tools and nails and whatever else was needed to further the destruction of the forest.

A strange numbness came over me. My body felt muffled, my breath constricted, as though I were being squeezed. I walked to the far end of the now barren clearing, winding between flesh-colored stumps, and stood at the edge of the woods, unsure just where I was in relation to the cedar tree. Everything was out of order, violated, and I could sense a layer of chaos gathering around me. I made myself thicker. Those spirits were coming. They wanted something.

A sudden nausea rose up, and the clearing turned into a blur. I knelt and coughed up the hot cocoa Ma had made for me in the kitchen the night before. I used my coat sleeve to wipe my mouth, and the sour smell grabbed hold of me — pulled me to the bare ground at the edge of the clearing, head spinning, breath heavy and deep, as though I were trying to keep from drowning.

Hard to describe the whirl inside — a storm of grief and fire, flashes of memory that weren't mine, and the palpable sense of spirits all pushing on me, wanting to show me something. A picture flashed of the whole forest cut and turned into a shopping mall with an enormous parking lot. The picture multiplied and I saw it cover the earth until all the trees were gone. I lay in this whirl, unable to move, as though my body had sunk into the ground.

The first bird sung. The sound was so vivid that it pierced clean through. A movement caught my eye, and I lifted my head. From under the tarp where the wood was piled came a weasel. He stood on his hind legs looking intently into the woods at my left, which I recognized now as the grove ruled by the old cedar. I heard a rustle, and a buck emerged from those trees, ears twitching. I saw him for just a moment before he shot across the clearing in a fiery blur, right passed the weasel, who dove under the tarp for cover. The dry branch from the old cedar lay near my hand.

I felt a rumbling. Those spirits were there. I could almost hear them whispering, urging me, pressing at my body to sit up, and so I did. My head had stopped spinning, but it felt loose on my neck. The weasel poked his head from under the tarp. I could see the edge of the pallets that held the stacked wood. Plenty of space under there for kindling.

I stood, cedar in hand, and walked toward the weasel, who dashed into the cedar grove. It was as if someone else knelt my body there, where the weasel had been; someone else used my hands to untie the ends of the tarp. Someone else broke up the dry branch and worked the pieces into the opening under the pallet. They were all there, those spirits, inside me and all around me. I lit a match. The dry cedar branch went bright, and I watched as the fire licked the pallet. Already it had caught on one edge.

I left by way of the cedar tree, stopping there only long enough to put my hand on its trunk. I felt it as a person, whole and real as though Aunt Marie were standing there. Then I ran through the woods toward the cemetery, toward the grotto, out of the trees and down the cement path that stretched the length of the convent. There, I slowed to a walk. The sisters were singing their morning prayers, and out of that sound came a hum from my own throat. I'd gone a long block before I realized it was Aunt Marie's song that I hummed.

SOMEHOW, I SENSED the fire had done exactly what it was supposed to, what with the spirits directing, so I went straight home from school and planned to make my visit to the woods in the darker hours. When I came in through the back door, Ma stood at the kitchen stove frying onions. The store-bought hamburger buns piled at her elbow were still in their plastic wrappings.

"Good that you came straight home," she said. "I could use your help with this. Union men coming tonight for a big meeting at 5:30 and we've got to feed them this time. Only have but an hour or so to get all this food prepared. How about you cut some onions for me?"

I dropped my schoolbooks at the edge of the counter. Ma handed me a knife and a wooden board, and I set to peeling and cutting, releasing the strong brew of onion into my eyes and throat until I was crying those strange, empty tears that only onions can bring.

Soon, the front door clicked open and we heard the sound of voices, one of them Pa's. They were arranging chairs, moving things around. By the time Ma and I finished cooking and brought the sloppy joe and burger buns on trays to the dining room, the front of the house was filled with men and an electric buzz of conversation. The dining room table was pushed against the wall where the portraits of Pa's parents hung.

As we set up the buffet, I glanced up and noticed a man in pinstripe trousers with shiny shoes, jangling the change in his pocket. I knew him right away from his pallid face and red, unruly eyebrows — I had seen him the day before at the driveway into St. Francis woods. At that time, he had been wearing a white hard hat, which hid his crew cut and long-lobed ears, but I was sure it was him because of the way his legs seemed to curve and dangle out of his hips as though he were riding a horse, even though he stood on his own feet. Not many people hold themselves up like a cowboy on a phantom horse. Something about him I didn't trust.

The man Pa had called Eddie walked over and shook the cowboy's hand, leaning in close to say something private. Then he took the serving spoon from the sloppy joe and banged it against the side of the pot. He didn't seem to notice that he had sent a spray of brown spots over Ma's good tablecloth. I went to the kitchen and wet the end of a dishrag to clean them up. By the time I got back to the dining room, the men had quieted, all eyes on Eddie. The cowboy stood by himself a few feet from Eddie's elbow, then moved away and leaned against the wall next to the kitchen door.

"We've had some developments that may change our plans for the strike on Monday," Eddie said. "Seems there's been a slow down in work at the Kroemer convent site. Meant to start stump removal today, but vandals set fire to the lumber stack and most of it burned to ash. The fire spread to the storage shed and destroyed the chipper machines."

I felt a redness creep up my neck — fear jump into my throat. I turned toward the kitchen door, dishrag in hand. There stood the cowboy and I had to go right passed him. I hesitated. Did he recognize me, from the other day? Is that why he was here? Maybe they knew — or at least suspected. I must have been staring because the cowboy turned and looked right into my face. I looked away, then rushed passed him into the kitchen.

"The fire is something of a help," I heard Eddie say as I closed the kitchen door. "Gives us one less site to picket. Only trouble is they think the union set the fire, and they're watching us close now." I stayed by the door to listen from the other side. I could feel the cowboy there — almost taste his breath.

"Could put Hoover in jeopardy if we have to wait later than Monday for the strike," I heard Pa say. There was a general roar in the room, and I heard the serving spoon against the pot again.

"What's so interesting about that union business?" I heard Ma say from the kitchen sink. "Can't see as how it'd be any concern of yours."

"Of course not, Ma. Just worried about your table-cloth," I said, heartbeat quickening, and busied myself at the kitchen table, cleaning up what was left of the onions. From there, I could make out little of what was said, though the cigar smoke had no trouble reaching us.

"We'll bleach the tablecloth good when the meetings are all over," Ma said, walking past me at the table, "though I don't know how we'll get that cigar stink out of the house." With that, she swung open the back door and a gust of cool air blew in, sending the last of the onion peels like fluttering moths to the linoleum floor.

I LEFT THE HOUSE BEFORE DAWN. The sky was barely luminous when I entered the front gate of the convent and stepped into St. Francis woods, passing the grotto, then cutting through the trees to the edge of the cedar grove where the desolate clearing of tree stumps remained. Already, they had begun to construct a chain-link fence at the edge of the clearing: aluminum posts stood in a row on the longest side, and holes were dug for more posts where the fence would round a corner and edge the trees.

I walked the trees' edge toward the spot where I had set the fire, and from that distance I could see what was left: a heap of ash with a few remnants of wood sticking up like blackened bones. The remains of the storage shed had already been removed, and a few mangled machines sat together in the ashes. The fire had done more than I had imagined possible with only that one bough of cedar for kindling, but of course, I had no way of knowing just what those spirits had done to help it along.

Standing at the edge of the cedar grove, I could feel the spirits gathering around me, buzzing against my skin, making a burn in my eyes that told me where to look: A bulldozer was now parked at the other end of the clearing. In the dim light, it had a monstrous appearance, its front jaws opened like teeth. The new fence stretched alongside it with a whirl of barbed wire over the top. They had wasted no time — by the end of the day, likely the whole area would be enclosed with that fence.

I moved gingerly along the trees, as though I could wake that fanged monster, then stood beside the back tire, which went almost to my shoulder. From there, I looked toward the clearing. The fence ran close to the cedar grove, and I saw how endangered was that ground, for according to the drawing I'd studied on the sign the day before, the store would go well beyond the area meant for the auto repair shop. It was clear to me now that the cedar grove would not be safe.

The spirits were thickening now, murmuring, directing. They knew what to do: urged me to a squat at the back of the bulldozer, showed me the tailpipe. *Stuff it with something. Block it good.* I went into the pines and collected two of the largest cones I could find, leaving prayers as offerings instead of tobacco, then slid those cones into the pipe. They fit snug, as though made for this purpose, and when I went to get a stick to push them in further, I saw in the damp oak leaves a red rubber ball. I had to push it hard to get it into the pipe, which meant it was perfect—a tight cap. I pushed it deep into the bowels of the monster with my stick.

I had done all of this with a stealthy efficiency, my mission finished before I even had a thought about what to do, and it was still early — still safe to be there, looking about, seeing what I could see. I came around to the other side of the bulldozer, thinking to scan the area for clues of what to do next. And suddenly — the shock of a dog's angry bark and a large german shepherd lunged toward me, chain unraveling behind him. I heard a truck door slam as I turned and ran toward the cedar grove, the dog snarling at my heels.

"Hey!" I heard a voice call. "Stop right there."

I kept running down the deer path into the grove of trees until my hands pressed into the trunk of the cedar and I leaned my cheek into the bark, breath heavy, sure as a child against her mother. We weren't alone: the spirits were there with us — a bold army. I turned my head, eyes toward the forest floor, and saw a pair of work boots, partially laced, coming toward me.

I didn't know it at the time, but those boots belonged to Jesse. This is what I don't understand: how in an instant, the whole course of my life could change.

9

POCKETS
HEAVY
WITH
POTATOES

Charlotte

JESSE GRASPED THE CHAIN of the growling dog, giving him a short leash as he walked toward me. He had chiseled features and deep blue eyes, dark hair sticking up on one side, rumpled sweatshirt, loose-fitting jeans. His gait had a bit of a swagger, but there was something vulnerable underneath the air of toughness. It seemed as though I'd gotten him out of bed.

"Hey," he said, sharply. "What are you doing here?"

"I help Sister Clare with the gardening," I said, hugging my arms.

"Long way from the garden."

"I like to visit this tree." Strange, how calm I felt there — as though just being under the cedar's limbs made me safe. I pressed my back against the trunk with a curious sense of abandon.

"It's an old one, alright," he said. "But you were over in the construction area."

"Just curious and went to have a look."

"You'll need to stay out of that area," he said. His voice had an edge, but his eyes were soft, and his posture had lost its armor.

"Sorry I spooked your dog," I said softly. "What's his name?" I knelt down on one knee and held out the back of my hand. The dog growled a little, then sniffed my glove. The smell seemed to calm him.

"It's okay, Bo," he said, stroking the dog's head. He squatted beside him. "Bo's not really a guard dog. He wouldn't have hurt you."

Now we were both petting the dog, scratching behind his ears, and up close, I could see that this man was barely a man. He couldn't have been more than a few years older than me — I was close to 17 at the time. Honestly, I'd never been that close to a man before, other than Pa. Something both rugged and boyish about him that I found appealing, and I felt something new, something pitched and electric between us.

"I'm Jesse," he said, holding out his hand. "And you?"

"Charlotte." I held out my hand in return, the white prom glove nearly glowing in the early morning light. His hand easily wrapped around mine. He pressed at the empty fingertip of my glove with the end of his thumb.

"What happened here?"

"Frostbite," I said, and he laughed.

"You go out in the dark *and* in the cold. Can I see?" He yanked at the end of my glove. I pulled my hand away and put it in my coat pocket.

"Nothing to be embarrassed about," he said. "I'm just curious."

I looked away, a deep fluttering in my belly, like dread and hope all swirling together. I didn't like it at all. "I should go," I said, and stood up.

He took hold of my sleeve, still squatting next to the dog. "Didn't you say you were curious about the construction? I can show you around."

He stood then, and unloosed the dog chain. "Go on, Bo," he said. And before I could say anything else, he grabbed my hand and pulled me along beside him as the dog ran ahead.

"Over there is where the auto shop goes. There'll be a parking lot here with lots of space to leave cars. Usually auto shops have a problem with that, so it'll be good. And over there?" He pointed toward the cedar grove. "The back end of the department store, where they'll warehouse merchandise."

I stopped, then, with an abruptness that forced him to stop, and the dog jolted on his chain. "What about the old cedar?" I said.

He looked puzzled.

"The tree we were just at. Will they cut it down?"

"They'll have to — the warehouse is going there," he said. "They plan on clearing that whole area, all the way to the front sidewalk."

I had already suspected this, but hearing him say it so casually was more than I could take. I felt my eyes fill, my breath get short. "I have to go," I said under my breath, and pulled my hand from his.

"You're upset." His voice was gentle. He was behind me now, a hand on my shoulder. I tried to shake his hand away, but he tightened his grip.

"Is it the old tree?"

I didn't answer. He peered into my face, so close I felt

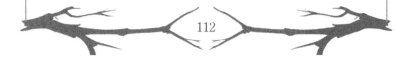

his breath on my cheek, the tiny breeze from his lips moving right through my skin. I felt disoriented, as though the world were melting.

"Why don't you come back to the truck? I have some hot cocoa in a thermos."

And before I knew what had happened, his arm lay dense and real around my shoulder and we were walking together between the stump wounds in the clearing, passed the pile of ash, passed the mangled machines, passed the bulldozer — my eyes full and spilling, our legs touching as we walked.

WHEN WE GOT BACK to the truck, Jesse unhooked the chain from Bo's collar. "Go get your ball, Bo," he said. The dog ran off into the trees while Jesse climbed into the cab of the truck. He emerged a moment later with a green thermos. The dog came back, running in a circle, wagging his tail.

"Where's your ball, Bo?" Jesse said. "Go get your ball."

The dog came to me then and put his nose in my hand, sniffing at my glove. I thought of the red ball I'd just stuffed into the exhaust pipe of the bulldozer, and my heart quickened. I tried to pet Bo's head to take attention away from the glove, but he kept nosing my hand, smelling.

"He must like you," Jesse said, as he poured the cocoa. "Usually nothing will distract him from playing ball."

He took a sip of the cocoa, then handed me the cup. The dog pushed his nose at my arm, again going for my glove. Jesse grabbed him by the collar.

"Sit!" he said, and the dog sat.

"Sorry," Jesse said. "Don't know why he's doing that. It's not like him."

I put my hand in my pocket. "I have to go anyway."

"Don't let him scare you off," Jesse said. "I won't let him bother you."

"I have to go to school."

"I can give you a lift in half an hour. That's when I get off."

"It's not far," I said. "I can walk."

"You ever come here in the evenings? Because I'll be back tonight at seven. I'll be doing a 12-hour shift. Gets pretty boring."

He took a step toward me, close enough that I could feel his heat, as though he carried inside the warmth of a hearth.

"Thanks for the cocoa," I said, and handed him the cup. Then I turned and walked quickly toward the cedar grove, his gaze steady on my back.

"See you tonight then," Jesse called after me. I turned and waved. He stood beside the truck: one hand wrapped with Bo's chain, the other holding the mug of cocoa. From this distance, he seemed no more solid than the spirits in the cedar grove, and I let my walk turn into a run.

I HADN'T BROUGHT my science book along with me to the woods, so I came home from school at lunch. When I stepped into the back porch, I heard voices in the kitchen and looked through the window. I was surprised to see Pa at the sink washing a bowl when he should have been at work. Ma sat at the table clipping coupons from the news-

paper and placing them in a chipped green bowl. The air felt thick with tension. I stood outside the door, not sure if I should go in.

"My Pa won't live forever, you know," I heard Ma say. She added another coupon to the green bowl. "Doctor says his heart's giving out. Just seems to make sense to go now. Won't be but a couple of days." She stopped her clipping and looked toward Pa. He wiped his hands on the flour sack towel, then slipped on his jacket without looking at her.

"You been so busy with the union, a little break would do us all good," Ma said.

"Seeing that family of yours ain't my idea of a break. And besides, it ain't the time. Charlotte's got school, and I don't know yet what'll happen this week."

"Then maybe I should go on my own and ask Belle to come along. Won't cost much for a couple of tickets, and we can stay with Ruthie."

"Meeting at the union hall tonight," Pa said, taking a brown bag from the counter. "Best not to expect me for supper."

"Won't need more than $30." Ma's voice had a tremor in it.

"I ain't paying for no train tickets," Pa's voice was stern. "Like I said, it ain't the time." He opened the back door and brushed past me, slamming the storm door behind him.

My eyes filled up. I had never seen Pa yell at Ma. I thought of Grandpa Abe standing on Aunt Marie's porch, smoking his pipe. That was the last time I'd seen him, on that visit to Aunt Marie's.

"Come inside and shut that door," Ma said, and she went back to her coupons. Her hands shook and her face was hard. "Don't be dawdling, now," she said without looking up. "You're going to be late getting back to school."

"Is Grandpa Abe okay?" I said to Ma.

"Just getting old," Ma said. "Same that happens to all of us."

"I'd like to see him," I said, even as I felt a kind of dread. I was afraid to go to the reservation again — afraid what contact with those spirits might do to me. I felt a sudden wave of nausea. The stale cigar smoke was too much. "My stomach hurts," I said, hoping Ma would let me spend the afternoon in bed.

Ma rubbed her eyes. "I have to go lay down. Vegetable soup on the stove — get yourself a bowl. If that doesn't settle your stomach, take a spoonful of coke syrup before you go." She pushed back her chair and walked out of the kitchen.

Never mind lunch. I retrieved my science book, got an apple from the refrigerator and left through the back door. When I came out of the gangway to the front sidewalk, a man in brown tweed pants and a coat too thin for the weather crossed the street and came right toward me.

"You Hayward Breton's girl?" The man asked.

I nodded. I noticed he wore shiny, expensive shoes.

"Could you do me a favor and give this to him?" He held out a small white envelope. H BRETON was printed in block letters across the front.

"Now you be sure he gets that by tonight, okay Doll?" the man said over his shoulder as he crossed the street. He got into the passenger seat of a black car and drove off. I ran back down the gangway and in the back door to leave the envelope for Pa. Seemed too important to risk losing it.

"That you, Charlotte?" I heard Ma say from her bedroom.

"Yes, Ma. Just leaving now." I laid the envelope on the dining room table.

"I'll be going to Belle's in a few minutes," she said, coming out of the bedroom. She was already wearing her black overcoat and a felt hat with a blue feather in one side. "Pa won't be back until late. There's a little of that sloppy joe left for your supper."

A car honked out front. "That'll be the taxi," she said. "I'll be back by nine." She picked up a tote bag from the end of the couch. I could see knitting needles sticking out the top, and the crossword book that Belle had forgotten the last time she visited. "Now don't be late for school. And don't forget your key."

"Okay Ma," I said, as the front door closed behind her.

I leaned against the table to think. Pa's relatives stared at me from their picture frames. Why weren't Ma's relatives up on that same wall? I thought of Grandpa Abe, Aunt Marie. It wasn't fair that their portraits weren't there, that Pa tried to stop Ma from visiting. I looked, then, at Grandma Breton in her Victorian collar, black hair piled high like a lady. She had died young, before I was born. Pa called her an angel. He said she was French, but her features were not European.

"She's not French, Pa," I whispered under my breath. "Your Ma was an Indian."

I DECIDED TO TAKE THE LONG WAY to school so I could check on the construction site. I would have preferred to go in through the trees where I wouldn't be seen, but there wasn't time, so I walked the sidewalk where the iron fence had been taken down. Already they had a new chain link fence across the front, complete with barbed wire. A long gate was open at the driveway and a large truck with a bulldozer on its flat trailer sat at the entrance. I couldn't tell if they were bringing a new one or removing the one that had been there last night. I slowed as I walked around the truck, looking into the gate to see what I could see. The fence was almost completed — at least towards the front — and it was not even one o'clock yet. They worked fast.

I looked up at the bulldozer and recognized that monster: the teeth were open in the same frozen grimace. Likely they'd have another one there by the end of the day. The rubber ball had done the job, but I didn't have any more of those. Then I remembered: Ma had two boxes of potatoes stored in the basement. I could find some the same size as the ball.

I ran home as fast as I could and found four of those potatoes, a handful of used nails to scatter in the dirt driveway and then on a whim, I grabbed a tube of glue with a narrow spout. I didn't know how I'd use it yet, but something told me it would come in handy.

AFTER SCHOOL, I went to St. Francis woods, my pockets heavy with potatoes. I stopped at the grotto, feeling suddenly weak. For so many years, I had been alone in those woods with only the spirits for company. Now out of nowhere, I was in the middle of this drama, completely unprepared. I looked up at Mary, blue robes flowing around her legs, palms open in a blessing. She seemed far away. I laid my belly on the ground in front of her, ignoring the cold. Something so comforting about that piece of earth, so familiar. My eyes got heavy and I was pulled down to where the sounds went white. I lay in between worlds, drifting, for a long time. When I finally sat up, the sun was low enough for me to make my way toward the construction site by way of the cedar grove to see what I could see.

I walked the deer paths, hidden by brush from the new fence, peering through the trees as the world went twilight. Somehow, they had finished the entire fence but for one length of it that faced the cedar grove. It looked as though that area was meant to have a wide gate like the one that spanned the front driveway — confirmation that they intended to pave there.

I heard a dog bark and so I squatted, kept still. Could it really be seven already? I crept along the edge of the site, hidden by the trees, until I could see Jesse's truck through the new chain-link fence. He was talking to the cowboy — I guessed he was Jesse's boss. There was another man there too who I recognized immediately: the man with the shiny shoes who had given me the letter for Pa. He was laughing, and then he put his arm around Jesse's shoulders and gave him a squeeze. They seemed real comfortable together. The cowboy gave Jesse a ring of keys — he seemed to be telling him what each one was for, pointing to a gate and then to a metal storage shed that now stood by the clearing. The three of them walked up the drive together, out of sight, and I heard a car start up.

"C'mon, Bo," I heard Jesse say. Then the dog ran into the clearing and retrieved a stick. They were playing. I didn't know yet what I would do, so I stayed there in the trees and surveyed the changes. There was a new bull-dozer — it had a different logo painted on the door — and the metal storage shed with a van parked beside it. I would need a smaller potato for that van. The fence made my work harder — anything I did would surely be heard by Jesse, unless I waited until he fell asleep, and that would mean coming back in the middle of the night. Already dark-ness had descended and with it, an icy wind.

"Here, boy," Jesse said. I heard the rattle of Bo's chain and their shadows moved together toward the pick-up. The truck door squeaked and then a tinny sound that must have been a transistor radio. No point in making a move now. I crept down the deer path so as not to alert Bo, dropped the potatoes behind the cedar tree and headed home, all the while making a list in my head of the things I would need to bring back: a flashlight, a warm blanket, an assortment of potatoes.

WITH MY SUPPLIES PACKED and ready, hidden in a corner of the back porch, I lay on my bed, hugging my pillow, aware of each tick of the clock. I would bring everything to the cedar tree, make that my base. I pictured Bo, and added to my supply list some dried jerky that Ma had made from a side of beef. Seemed something a dog would like. My mind invented scenario after scenario and it was tiring me out. I still had a long time to wait: Ma and Pa had to be well asleep before I could go.

Ma got home first. The house was so quiet that even from the attic I could hear the sound of her tote bag landing on the couch, the tinkling of her knitting needles. Some time passed, and then a key jiggled in the lock and the front door closed with a little bang. The murmur of voices, and the attic door swung open, sending a waft of air up the stairwell.

"Charlotte? Come down here," Pa said from the foot of the steps. His voice was firm, urgent.

I set the pillow aside, afraid he had found my supplies. I went downstairs, legs rubbery on the steps. Pa stood at the dining room table holding the white envelope in his hand.

"Do you know how this got here?" Pa waved the envelope.

"A man gave it to me."

"What man? When?"

"After lunch, on the way back to school," I said. "He told me to give it to you by tonight, but you were already gone."

Pa's face went pale. Ma came in from the kitchen and stood behind me.

"Did he say his name?" Pa asked.

I shook my head. I could feel Ma's hands rest on my shoulders.

Pa looked down at the note. His hands shook. Then he looked back at me, his face fierce and hard, frightened.

"Don't you be talking to no men, you hear me? You'll

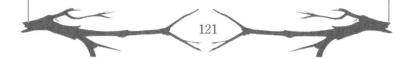

be staying inside this weekend, less me or your Ma are with you, understand?"

"Hayward, don't frighten her," Ma said. "She's done nothing wrong."

"Ain't about that," Pa said. "Just want to be on the safe side. From the looks of this note, them bosses got tipped off. I best go call the union boys and let them know."

PA STAYED ON THE PHONE a long time with those union men, calling this one, then that one, pacing the dining room, and so it was well after midnight by the time I got to the edge of the forest clearing, pockets filled with potatoes, sturdy stick in hand. A clear, cold night with the moon nearing its zenith meant I didn't need the flashlight to find my way to the new bulldozer. I worked quickly, got the potato deep inside, then moved onto the van. I had guessed well on the size of its tailpipe, which I had based on the neighbor's van: my selection of potatoes were all close in size, and one fit just right.

All was going smoothly, until I pulled the stick out of the pipe after my last good shove and banged the bumper. Immediately, the sound of Bo's chain, his snarling bark, the slam of the truck door. I moved quickly to the opening in the fence and tossed the stick into the trees. Bo was already nearing and I could see Jesse's flashlight bobbing across the clearing. I reached into my pocket for a handful of beef jerky.

"Here Bo," I said, kneeling down and holding out my hand.

Bo sniffed at my mitten and happily took the jerky. I

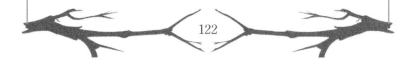

scratched him behind the ears, then stood up.

"It's just Charlotte," I called to Jesse, his shadow growing larger, the bobbing light landing on tree wound after tree wound.

"Charlotte?" He called back, incredulous, like it was some sort of miracle.

"I came back to visit." Strange, that I didn't feel nervous at all. It was as though someone else were speaking through my mouth, someone who knew just what to say.

"I know it's late," I said, as Jesse approached under a sky thick with stars. "But I was lying in my warm bed and something told me you needed a blanket."

Bo nuzzled my hand, looking for another piece of beef jerky, then licked my mitten, as though tasting the smell left in the fabric.

Jesse looked puzzled. "A blanket?"

"You're only wearing a sweatshirt," I said. "Wait here."

I slipped into the cedar grove and went to the mother tree where I had dropped the blanket on my way in. There, I emptied my pockets of potatoes and hid them in a dense heap of brown cedar needles, then took off the mittens that smelled of the tailpipe and stuffed them into my pockets, leaving only my prom gloves. When I got back with the blanket, Jesse was still standing in the same spot, flashlight pointed down. I draped the blanket over his shoulders. A shiver seemed to run through him.

"You didn't even realize you were so cold," I said as I adjusted the drape to keep the ends from dragging.

"You're right, I didn't." He looked into my face as though searching for something. "It's so late," he said.

"I know. But I couldn't sleep, knowing you would be so cold." As soon as I said it, I knew it was true. My eyes filled up. I didn't know until that moment: this was the reason I had brought the blanket.

10

VIEW FROM THE PICKUP

Charlotte

I WAS SURPRISED by how easy it was to fall in with Jesse, sneaking out after Ma and Pa were asleep. We liked to cuddle on the hood of his truck wrapped together in the wool blanket and sip hot cocoa while we watched the moon wander the sky, leaving its puddles of dappled blue light under the trees. Something so easy between us — as though we'd known each other all our lives.

Being there each night, it was easy to monitor the changes in the construction site. The work had slowed considerably after those first few days. Jesse told me they got a couple of bum bulldozers and they were on a waiting list for another. They were having trouble finding the equipment they needed after all the chipper machines were destroyed in the fire. Then the carpenters had gone on strike, soon joined by the pipe fitters, the electricians and finally, the glass cutters. So the work ground to a halt, the project put on hold so they could concentrate on other sites that were further along given the shortage of labor. Jesse was just there to be sure there was no foul play on the part of the unions until it was all resolved and work could begin.

I learned other things, too. That the man with the shiny

shoes was his Uncle Roy — a lawyer whose firm had a contract with the Kroemer Brothers — and he had gotten Jesse a number of jobs on their projects. Jesse's mom had died in the fall, so now Jesse was alone, since he had no father. He was having trouble concentrating in his classes, so he dropped out of college for the semester. He would have rather been doing construction again, as he had the previous summer, but this job would have to do until the strike was over. Jesse said he might not be able to do construction anymore for Kroemer because of those unions. It made him mad.

Jesse liked to talk while I listened. I liked his boldness — how he seemed willing to tell me anything. What he actually said wasn't as important as what I could feel underneath — some of it so tender that it would be impolite to say anything about it, but he could sense that I knew and sometimes it made him nervous. All the while, we stayed cozy inside our wool cocoon. Now and then, Jesse would start the pick-up and let the engine run until the heat rose under the hood. I liked the feeling of that warm metal surface vibrating under us as I sat between his legs and leaned back against his chest, his breath in my hair, his palms resting on my belly. I had never been so physically close to another person before and some neglected part of me crept out of hiding to soak up the nourishment of it.

A couple of times, Jesse fell asleep on the hood, and I made good use of those moments. He kept the key ring in his jacket pocket, so I was able to open the storage shed and add grit to the oil they stored there for the machines, and then glue their lids in place. I figured this would at least slow them down when they started work again. I was careful to use an old pair of Ma's garden gloves while I did this so any smell would be contained, and kept those stuffed deep in the pocket of my coat. I smeared my hands with the rose-scented lotion Belle had given to me to mask any residual smells before going back to Jesse.

Of course, it was only a matter of time before Jesse found his way inside my clothes. At first, he just unbuttoned my coat so we could lay chest to chest and warm each other, sweet and tender. Then one night, he slid his hand up under my sweater and kept it in the crook of my back, his breath quickening, an electric intensity in his fingertips, his lips moving over my neck, heat of his breath going cool in the wetness he left. I stiffened when he did these things—something about the way he did it seemed not to include me.

One windless night, the blue light of the full moon emboldened me, and I coaxed Jesse away from the truck to show him the other part of the forest. The moon was so bright, we didn't need a flashlight, especially seeing as I knew those deer paths so well. It was warmer than usual, unseasonably so, and the air teased us with the promise of spring, but Jesse still brought along the wool blanket, just in case. I showed him the stand of pines I liked to visit and the hyacinths I'd planted for Sister Clare near the grotto, their scent rising strong in the night air. We bent down to smell them and to touch the little green spears coming up where the crocuses were just beginning to stir underground.

I wanted to show him the graveyard, but he said he'd

rather not go there at night, so we spread the blanket out under the stand of birch near the grotto where we could smell the hyacinths. We lay beside each other, air so still and sweet, the light from the moon making magic through the bare tree limbs, painting a complex web of elegant blue light and shadow on the ground.

"Don't you get lonely," Jesse asked, "spending so much time here?"

"Not lonely. The forest is like a person. I love this place more than anywhere."

"You can't really say more than anywhere. You don't know other places. It's a big world."

"The big world is more beautiful than this forest?"

"Not tonight." He buried his face in my hair. "You know me better than anyone," he whispered, and I could feel his body relax in a way I hadn't felt before. That made me relax, too.

It was after midnight. The moon had shifted higher, making paintings through the pines onto our bodies, the stillness broken only by the sound of the owls calling each other from high in the trees. Jesse let out a deep sigh. And then something flowered and let go — melted into the night. No need of edges in this stillness, even as we were more alive and real than ever before, the contentment so deep and pervasive, so complete, so without time, I can only call it God.

We lay together for what felt like a long time in that luminous, unbounded rapture. Then Jesse wrapped the blanket over me and I drifted into a light, dreamless sleep. I woke when I felt him adjusting the blanket, lying against

me, pulling me to his chest. Still edgeless and opened, I felt a shard of fear come off him in the darkness. It seemed tiny as a gnat, not enough to matter in this place we had entered, and I drifted back to sleep. Then all at once, that fear changed to fire and before I knew what was happening, he moved on me with an intensity that I hadn't seen in him before, his breath heavy, hands moving over my body with a greed that frightened me. I pushed against his shoulders but that just seemed to quicken him, so I stopped pushing and looked up into the sky. The arms of the trees held my spirit until there was a thick padding between Jesse's touch and my skin.

I felt something, then, between my legs, a strange, heavy sensation, something pushing, tearing at me. He grabbed me tighter, his hips moving fast as the tears seeped from my eyes and I felt my bones go limp. Then my spirit soared above the trees and dissolved into space.

Jesse stopped moving as suddenly as he had started, breath heavy. "So good," I heard him say from far away, "so good." I felt a cold wetness on the blanket, a sticky liquid seeping out of me, running off my thigh. How could he not notice that I had gone numb with fear and confusion? How could he have called this good?

His breathing changed. Now he was sleeping. I untangled myself from him as carefully as I could, did up my clothes and my coat, made my way to the path that led to the front gate, and ran through the trees — passed the graveyard, passed the convent with its sleeping sisters — all the way home.

I STAYED AWAY from the construction site after that, only going by the front driveway every few days during lunch break to be sure nothing had changed. Since Pa had organized the strike, he wasn't allowed to go to work, and the union men didn't want him on any of the picket lines. They warned him to stay near home as sometimes these things could get unexpectedly violent, and they didn't want him scapegoated by the bosses. So Pa was home most days, alone and restless in the living room, caged and impatient, getting more and more nervous about money as the days wore on with no salary being earned. Sometimes the union men would come by for a strategy meeting, but it seemed they didn't need him so much, now that the strike was underway. I didn't like being home with Pa in that stressful state. It stirred up my belly too much, and I would have preferred to be in the woods, but I didn't want to risk running into Jesse, so after school, I helped Ma with the spring gardening, then went to my attic room to ruminate over what had gone wrong with the woods, with Jesse, with Pa, with the world.

A few weeks went by like this. Then one day, I was walking home from school, crossing the street right near my house, when I heard someone call my name. I turned and there was Jesse, leaping out of the cab of his pickup, coming toward me, a look on his face so grieved that it hurt me to see it.

"Charlotte, what happened? Where did you go? I've been looking everywhere for you." He took my hand, his face open and sad, and I saw in him a loneliness so hollow and wretched that I kicked my pain aside in favor of his.

I could see his eyes register what I had just done and watched the vitality return to him, even as I suddenly felt drained of my own.

I heard the sound of the front door opening and pulled my hand away. "My Pa is coming out," I said. "I can't talk now."

As I walked away, I heard him say, "Please come tonight. I'll be waiting for you."

I felt his eyes on my back, like a claim, just as his cowboy boss stepped onto the front porch of my house and looked up the street toward Jesse's truck, then at me as I headed down the gangway toward the back door. What was he doing there?

In the kitchen, Ma was cleaning jelly jars. The strong smell of cigar smoke wafted under the kitchen door.

"Leave your book bag here and go pick some of those early strawberries," Ma said without turning from the stove. "Your Pa's in the middle of an emergency union meeting. Could go until dinner."

I wanted to warn Pa about that cowboy. I suspected he was spying for Kroemer—-after all, I'd seen him talking to Jesse's Uncle Roy. But what could I say that would make sense to Pa? I was feeling nauseous and only wanted to go to my room, but I couldn't open the kitchen door until the men left, so I took a small basket from the porch and walked behind the house to the strawberry patch. The earth between the plants was padded with dry leaves and I crouched there, broken leaves sticking to my socks, and took my time choosing the strawberries, grateful to have something to focus on that would take my mind off Jesse.

I could still feel him, like an echo. The world had an unreal quality, and when that first wave of nausea came up, I felt as though I were underwater, the strawberry patch oddly out of place. But then the smell of the earth rose up in the damp air and brought me back. When the basket was full, I came up the back steps and could hear Pa talking from inside the kitchen.

"Them boys say it could be a couple of weeks before I can go back to work."

"Let's pray it gets settled sooner than that," Ma said.

"Best you skip your trip north," said Pa, "Seeing as how money will be tight."

"Belle's already paid for the tickets — can't be refunded. Once we arrive it won't be costing much, staying with family."

"Don't see what you want with spending a week away," Pa said. "Plenty to tend to around here."

"Four days," Ma said. "Haven't seen my family in almost seven years."

"You've got no business going off at a time like this."

"My staying back won't change those bosses minds. You got the time now, you can come along with."

"What do I want with those lazy Indians?"

I felt a pain in my belly that I shared with Ma. I wanted to shout at Pa that his own mother was Indian and he called her an angel, but I held my breath and waited. Ma banged something on the counter, then said sharply, "Make yourself useful and peel some potatoes."

"Ain't hungry," Pa said. I heard the kitchen door slam.

I pushed open the back door and put the basket on the table, then headed straight for the attic door.

"What about supper?" Ma said to my back.

"Not for me," I said, and went up the stairs. I laid on the bed in the dark and felt the tension from the argument twist around my thoughts of Jesse. As soon as I closed my eyes, I saw him drifting on a black sea, eyes full of grief, and a sudden weight settled on my body, my belly heavy and whirling, pushing me down into the black with him.

For three days I was nauseous and unwilling to eat, until finally Ma brought me to the doctor. She stood by the door while he examined me, then he ushered her into the waiting room while I got dressed. When he came back, he asked if there was any chance I could be pregnant because I sure had all the symptoms. I nodded, averting my eyes as the heat creeped up my neck. Thankfully he hadn't told Ma, just in case he was wrong. He took the blood he needed for the pregnancy test, gave me a small envelope of anti-nausea pills and said he'd call with the results.

When we got home, I took two of the nausea pills, then went straight up to my room and stood in the window that looked out over the yard, leaning against the window ledge to steady myself. It had been days since I wanted any food besides crackers, and my mind was spread wide into space, even as my stomach gripped itself with dread. Was there a baby inside me? The young leaves of the apple tree nearly touched the window and I could see something glimmering between them, heard faint murmurs that sounded like children. There were voices in the tree. They were saying prayers. I ran down the steps, through the kitchen where

Ma was already at work on her canning, and out the back door.

The limbs of the apple tree were low, easy to reach from the v-shaped trunk, and I hoisted myself high into the tree. I straddled a sturdy limb and leaned my belly into it, arms dangling, cheek against the bark. Faint streams of light danced between the branches. The children were chanting now.

I needed those prayers and so did Jesse. It was wrong, that this had happened — that he did what he did, that I didn't stop him. I mouthed my own prayer, but no sound came. Maybe if I sang loud enough inside my head, my voice would come. I tried, but nothing came, so I gave up and let the children do the praying, let their prayers sink into me, my own lips moving as though in a whisper, breathing only silent air. Voice or not, I had to say it. I had to let God know how sorry I was, but there just couldn't be a baby come through me.

Someone was saying my name. I opened my eyes, cheek still pressed against the tree limb. There below me was Ma, looking up, face stern with worry, voice gentle.

"Come down now, Charlotte. Please come down."

IN THE KITCHEN, a big pile of Ma's homegrown strawberries covered the table and the canning pot simmered on the stove. On the counter sat three glass jelly jars. Ma's hands rested on my shoulders, maneuvered me to a chair by the window. I sat as directed, then watched as she cleared a small area of the table in front of me and placed a bowl of cornmeal mush there. I hadn't thought anything of food until I smelled the butter melting over the warm cereal and lifted a spoon to my lips. Immediately I recognized the sharp pains in my stomach not as nausea, but as hunger. The phone rang in the living room. Ma wiped her hands on her apron, which was already smeared with strawberry juice.

"Put your spoon down between bites," Ma said as she left the room, "or you'll give yourself a bellyache all over again."

The cereal was too good. I tried to slow down and compromised by smelling each bite before I ate it. But then something in Ma's voice from the other room made me stop. I put down the spoon.

"I'm so sorry to hear that," Ma said quietly into the phone. "Thank you for letting me know."

Ma came back into the kitchen. She didn't look at me. I quivered inside with heat and dread while Ma took her time finishing the strawberries on her cutting board. I watched her adjust the flame under the pot, then move back to the table and pick up a particularly large berry. She sliced it open. Inside was the reddest red I had ever seen.

"A shame to cook this one," Ma said. She handed half of it to me without meeting my eyes. I put the strawberry in my mouth but couldn't taste a thing. I watched as Ma ate her's one small bite at a time. Then she wiped her hands on her apron, scooped up a handful of berries and put them on the cutting board. Her hands paused. Finally, she looked up at me, eyes full of hurt. Even before she said a word, I knew that Jesse's baby swam wild in my belly.

I heard Pa's key in the front door and pushed my chair

back so hard it fell. The danger pumped me full of power and I was in my coat and out the door before Ma could say anything but my name. I just started running hard and fast, not wanting to be there when she told Pa, already feeling his rage like a wolf at my heels. I meant to go to the grotto, but ran right passed it and through the woods to the fence at the far side of the construction site. Jesse wasn't there yet, so I sat with my back against a cedar, feet on the fence, and watched for his truck. I remember my head getting heavy, an icy wind coming with the dark, my mind thick with hunger and a hollowness that made me spread out through the trees. Fragments of dream, the murmur of spirits. Then Bo's nose, sniffing, fast breath on my cheek, someone saying my name, and when I opened my eyes, Jesse's face, full of alarm.

"There's a baby inside me," I said. I couldn't hold it any longer.

A wave of fear passed over his face. "You're shivering," he said. "When did you get here? We've got to get you to the truck, get you warmed up."

I remember him helping me through the gate and across the clearing to the truck. I remember the heat blasting, the crackers he gave me, the cup of warm cocoa, my eyes going heavy again.

THEN IT WAS MORNING, and I didn't know where I was. An unfamiliar bed, a hum that might have been a refrigerator. Someone was breathing beside me, a lump under the blanket sending off heat, like a rock warmed by the sun. The room smelled of dirty socks and in the dim light,

I could make out a pile of laundry in the corner. The morning sun leaked in from a transom over the door, and I could see Jesse's boots on the mat, brown laces twisted like skinny snakes. Something churned in my belly and a wave of nausea passed through. I curled my knees up to make it settle.

I remembered then, how I must have gotten there — how I left the house after Ma found out about the baby. Somehow I got up the stairs, into this bed. That, I don't remember—just the faint sense of Jesse's protective guilt.

The room was getting brighter and I could see better. A kitchenette in a curved cove. A clock shaped like a rooster over the stove. Pushed against the wall outside the kitchen, a rickety oak table on spindle legs. Beside it, Jesse's jacket hung on the back of a wooden chair, his jeans draped over the seat. I was still fully dressed except for my jacket and boots, which lay in a pile beside the mattress within easy reach. I could put the jacket on now, I thought, while he was still asleep. I could slip out the door, put my boots on in the hallway. It would be so easy.

Another wave of nausea rose in me, and this one I couldn't push down. I slipped out of bed and went to the kitchen sink to throw up what little was in my stomach, but then I couldn't stop retching. Something was really off. Probably I was dehydrated and weak with hunger. I could feel Jesse moving from the bed, padding over to the kitchen.

"You okay?" He twisted the faucet away from my head, filled a glass halfway with water.

The retching stopped and I took some deep breaths,

hands still gripping the edge of the sink. My throat burned, but I felt better.

"How about a sip?" he said. I took the glass from him and leaned against the wall, still breathing hard. Jesse rinsed out the sink, sprinkled it with cleanser. He was wearing only a t-shirt. His bare legs must have been cold, but he didn't show it. I watched his shoulders work as he scrubbed the sink, rinsed the sponge and squeezed it out, then set it to dry on the counter. He turned toward me and I looked at his feet, solid on the grey linoleum floor as though held there by a magnetic force that didn't apply to me.

"You should lay down," he said. But I shook my head and took another sip of water. He studied my face and for a moment we were both lost and foreign to each other. The room felt airless. I could hardly breathe. I pulled back inside myself like a turtle and felt him move away from me, heard the rattle of his belt as he pulled on his jeans.

I put the glass on the counter and walked over to the mattress, picked up my jacket from the floor, slipped it on.

"If you're cold, I can give you a sweater," Jesse said. He was faking confidence, leaning against the threshold of the cove, eating an apple that he took from a glass bowl on top of the refrigerator.

"I have to go," I said as I picked up my boots.

"Where is there to go?"

I knew he was right, but I didn't like that he said it out loud. I walked to the door without looking at him, turned the lock and rattled the doorknob, but the door wouldn't open. I felt Jesse behind me, reaching up, unlatching a lock at the top of the door over my head. Now that he was

dressed, he smelled of the forest and the gasoline that must have spilled from the spout when he stopped to fill the truck. Another smell, too, that I remembered was always strongest by his neck — a smokiness that I only ever smelled on him. My hand paused on the doorknob.

"You can stay here," he said, as he put his arms around me from behind. My back was stiff against his chest, resisting his warmth. *No, no, no, no,* I was thinking. But his arms were settling around me, his face in my hair. He rested a hand on my belly.

"How's it feeling?"

"Ok," I said. But it wasn't true. I was queasy, and I could tell it would take diligence to keep the retching from coming back. Everything felt out of balance and I was afraid I had a fever.

"Come back to bed with me," he said. And suddenly, I felt him all around me, pulling me out of myself and into him. I tightened my grip on the doorknob. It took all I had to get myself back.

"I really have to go," I said, and somehow slipped out of his field and through the door. He followed me into the hallway. I could feel his eyes on my back as I walked toward the staircase, boots still in my hand.

"I have to work at seven," he said. "Meet me at the truck. I'll bring dinner." Something in his tone reminded me of Pa. As my foot touched the first step, I heard the door click shut behind him.

Once on the street, I saw that Jesse's apartment was the largest building on the block — a six flat. The rest were brick duplexes with a few scattered bungalows in between, squares of grass and neatly trimmed shrubs in front of each building. I didn't know where I was. I knew it couldn't be too far from St. Francis woods but nothing was familiar. I sat on the front steps to pull on my boots. It was cold out, but it would warm up when the sun was higher.

Another wave of nausea passed through me. I got on my knees, head in the bushes, thinking I might be sick, but the clean smell of the shrubs seemed to cure it. I wanted to go to the woods, to the grotto, but first I needed to lie down for just a minute, think this through. I curled up in a ball with my head near the juniper, the smell of earth and pine the closest I could get to home.

11

EXILED

Charlotte

SEVEN YEARS HAVE PASSED since Jesse and I stood in front of the judge with Ma standing behind us as witness, along with Jesse's Uncle Roy in his shiny dress shoes. I remember so little, just the loud tick of a clock on the wall, its brass pendulum swinging in staccato rhythm, drowning out the judge's words. He had to ask me twice, I was so far away. But then I said, "Yes, I do," and we were married.

Soon after, the baby left, just as I knew she would. Her spirit hovered, never entered, and what was to be her body slipped out of me in a clump, unneeded. But by then it was too late. Something was set in motion and there was no way to turn things back.

I don't know what happened to the forest, to the old cedar. I'm sure it's all gone now. And where did the spirits go? Do they haunt the department store warehouse, the auto shop? Sometimes I want to ask Jesse to take me there so I can feel for myself, but it's all so far away—the forest that was my home now just a dream I had long ago. When I get sad, Jesse still thinks I miss the house — the attic room where I slept, Ma in the kitchen making strawberry jam — and he gets mad all over again at Pa, who hasn't forgiven me for going with the nephew of the lawyer who nearly broke the strike. I can't say that I blame Pa. Taking his enemy into his family is asking a lot. When it was all over, Pa got his raise, though not as much as he'd hoped for, and he had a place in the union, but that wasn't enough to make up for it.

And now? I know what it is to be exiled. Here in this crumbling Victorian, this wooden shell of greed and privilege from the past — this is not my world. I'm living in someone else's world because of Jesse's hurt, how I saw it clearer and more urgent than my own, and how his skin against mine seemed to keep it at bay.

I long ago numbed from the pain of how absent he was from his own touch, and that left only what it had awakened in me — a deep longing for a union that I can feel in the body. Jesse and I haven't approached such union, but that doesn't change what I've come to suspect: that God is not in heaven after all, but right here, in my feet kissing the surface of the earth. Not the God of the church, or of myth, but that ineffable sense of space and tenderness that sometimes comes to me like a visitation, like the breeze that comes through the crack in the window — an invitation to life.

I often think of that night in the moonlit forest with Jesse before his fear rose up and drowned out the owls, brought back the sharp edges of things, estranged me from him. That place of melting where everything belonged seemed the whole reason we had come together. But after we married, he soaked himself through with the hardworking light of day, and in the years that followed, I couldn't find the Jesse I'd met when he still loved to be in the forest at night, air thick with the scent of pine. I thought he would

return eventually and go back there with me, but it's gone on so long that now I'm afraid we're lost to each other.

Even worse, he's lost to himself. And so am I.

My only consolation is the backyard. Other than the old oak, it's still mostly bare earth and brown grass, but I've been digging it up a bit at a time. As long as I'm here, I'll do what I can to bring it back. The oak is a beginning — the soul of that tree speaks to me like a grandfather, protector of life, broad leaf-covered arms giving shelter to the little plants until they can take hold amongst the deadness. And then there is the cedar sapling that Jesse got for me when we first moved in. He probably bought it from the nursery, but I don't want to ask. I like to think that it came from the cedar grove at St. Francis woods — a baby of that mother tree I knew so well. I like to think she lives on here, even in this little stick with its spindly branches.

It will be a tree some day. I'll see to that.

THE MORNING LATA WAS DUE to come, I got up early and went to the railroad tracks. Nearby there was an unkempt break of trees, mercifully wild, where I liked to look for plants, and I went there to dig up trilliums. I spent the rest of the morning in the backyard on my knees, hands wet with earth, turning it over with a hand trowel. Jesse bought me a shovel for this, but I never use it. To touch the earth is to know it. I can feel with my own hands which of the plants would be happiest there. Jesse told me that I could have the whole yard done in an afternoon if I used the shovel. He even offered to do it for me, but what good would that do? I wouldn't know any of it then.

I was patting the earth around a trillium when Belle drove up in her station wagon. I could hear the door creak when it opened. Jesse must have seen her arrive, because he was already at the car, helping her with Lata's suitcase and a grocery bag that probably had a casserole in it. Belle never seemed to go anywhere without a casserole. I pretended for a minute that I didn't hear them. I wanted to spend just a little more time with the trillium. It had only three leaves, and already a shy white bud hid under one of them.

I thought of the trilliums that came up along the path in St. Francis woods — the first time I discovered their flowers. I had walked by them so many times, wanting to go to my favorite places, and saw them just as leaves. But one morning the sun was coming through the trees and lit up one of the plants as though with a spotlight. I knelt down to admire the newness of the green, to touch it, and found its secret flower. That trillium taught me to get in close to every plant I meet, so I won't miss anything.

I stood and rubbed my hands together to brush the dirt off, then lifted the watering can to sprinkle the trillium I just put in, the smell of earth rising all around it. I breathed in deep. No smell satisfies so much as wet earth.

"Charlotte," I heard Jesse say, and looked up. He was on the other side of the picket fence holding a grocery bag. A lock of dark hair fell on his forehead. I felt him more as a force than a person, pulling me out of my own feet, my own world, into the one that he and Belle agreed on. I put the watering can on the ground and walked to the gate, stopping to scrape my bare feet against the crack in the concrete walkway to get the mud off. Jesse had already

gone into the house with the grocery bag, so I walked over to the station wagon.

Belle was leaning deep into the car, and I could hear grocery bags rustle against her chest as she reached over them. She emerged with a box of graham crackers and brushed her hand over the skirt of her floral dress.

"Lata is a good girl," Belle said to me. "A little shy. She won't get in your way." She looked past me, her face shifting into the familiar mask she wears when uncomfortable — smile a little too wide, eyes a little too bright. "Lata honey," she said, "come get your graham crackers and show Aunt Charlotte your new haircut."

Lata was standing next to the paper birch, her fingers absently stroking the bark. Her hair was cut short — just below her ears — and the bangs were a little crooked.

"I cut it myself," Belle said. "I saw in *Good Housekeeping* how I could get this style by putting a bowl on her head so it would come out perfectly even. Isn't it cute?"

Lata tugged at a lock of hair as though trying to make it grow back, her face placid. Under her solemnity, I sensed something dormant in her — a seed that needed tending.

I heard the screen door slam and Jesse bounded down the stairs, across the lawn and over to Lata. "I've got your room all ready for you," he said. "Want to see?"

Lata nodded. Jesse scooped her up into his arms. How solid she was, lithe and strong — like a cat. I watched Jesse carry her toward the back door. Lata looked over his shoulder and met my gaze.

I saw in her, then, the seed of fire. It was Aunt Marie's. It was my own.

148

12

THE

DANGER

OF

BOOTS

Lata

UNCLE JESSE PUT ME TO BED as he had the night before. Even though he didn't stay long, I slept inside that night. I sensed that it would be better to wait a few days before returning to the hammock. Before dawn I heard his van back out of the garage. A few minutes later, my bedroom door creaked open and there was Aunt Charlotte, dark hair falling over her eyes, nuzzling my neck like a puppy. She was already dressed in an olive green t-shirt with a hole at the hem. An old pair of Uncle Jesse's jeans hung loose from her hips.

"Come on, Lata," she said. "I have things I want to show you today."

A storm was brewing. The temperature had dropped and the wind rattled at the window. I did not want to get up.

Aunt Charlotte tossed my clothes from the day before onto the bed. "Hurry, Lata, we have a long way to go."

Outside, the sky had a smear of light and the streetlights had started to flicker. She walked fast toward the garage and I followed behind. Aunt Charlotte didn't like to drive and rarely went anywhere that she couldn't get to on foot. Uncle Jesse always drove his work van, so the old blue mustang hadn't been driven since May. She had to lift the hood and poke at something with a ballpoint pen to get it to turn over. The muffler coughed out a vile smoke.

"Where are we going?" I asked, as she loaded the back seat with a bundle of newspaper and some gardening supplies. "Can't we walk?"

"It's a surprise," Aunt Charlotte said, "and it's too far to walk." She unlocked the door and I climbed onto the vinyl seat.

By the time the sun was up, the landscape had changed to neat farms and white fences. Now that the storm had cleared and the car was beginning to run smoothly, I was glad we were driving. I had never before moved through this much of the world so early in the morning. After a while, I started to get hungry and announced this to Aunt Charlotte.

"I thought we'd go on a little fast together," she said. "That means we won't eat, but we can get some water when we stop for gas."

She stopped at a place called Earl & Son Gas Food. I went inside to find the restroom. On the counter, cardboard displays stood like family photos and held mostly key chains with car logos dangling from them. I spotted one chain with a small bit of white fur instead of a logo. I stroked it as you would a tiny kitten. Aunt Charlotte came in and paid for the gas.

"Could you buy this for me?" I asked, still stroking the fur.

She helped me wrestle it off the display and paid the cashier. As we walked back to the car, she asked if I knew what it was. I shook my head.

"It's a rabbit foot," she said. "They're supposed to be good luck."

I looked at the fur in my palm. "Not a real rabbit," I said as we got into the car.

"Yes, a real rabbit. When the rabbit dies they cut off its foot for good luck."

I dropped the fur into my lap. I couldn't touch it anymore, knowing where it had come from. I didn't see how such a thing could be lucky.

Aunt Charlotte started the car, then reached for the rabbit's foot.

"The rabbit would die anyway," she said. "This way the rabbit leaves behind some luck. That's not so bad, is it?" She hung the rabbit's foot from the rearview mirror. As we drove, it dangled and swung like a corpse.

BY LATE MORNING, we were on a two-lane road with forest on one side and shabby houses scattered along the other. The houses were surrounded by packed dirt instead of the lawns I was used to. A group of small, dark-haired children clustered on the barren earth, tossing a ball high into the air. Aunt Charlotte pulled the car over and the children stopped their game.

"I'll be just a minute. I need to get directions."

She walked between the children to the front porch and talked to someone through an aluminum screen door. By the time she walked back, the children had resumed their game and she glided around their circle, careful not to disrupt them.

We turned onto a narrow dirt road and suddenly were in

a thick forest. We drove for a while over the rugged road, and then Aunt Charlotte pulled the car onto a patch of dirt notched into the trees. When she switched it off, I could hear only the restless sound of fallen leaves. We walked down the road, my hand lightly linked to hers. It all felt strangely familiar, as though some lost memory had surfaced and I knew how it would feel to move through that sun-dappled wall of trees, walking so lightly that we'd leave no tracks, the forest closing behind us and opening before us.

We followed a curve in the road and came to a clearing filled with brittle cattails and tall, wheat-colored grass. At the edge of the clearing, surrounded by young poplars, stood a small farmhouse. Over the years, someone had built a crooked addition that was now as weathered as the rest of it, but without question, this was the farmhouse from Aunt Charlotte's photograph. Most of the windows were bare and reflected the light, but one had a shade with curled edges pulled low, and the door had a tattered curtain covering its window.

We turned onto a dirt path just wide enough for the two of us and walked toward the house. We had to wade through weeds dried and stiffened from the sun to get to the patch of bare earth in front of the door. Next to the porch, dead thistles stood like soldiers. Aunt Charlotte tried the door, but it was locked. A window just to her left had a loose board in place of glass. She pulled hard until the nails popped and leaned the board against the side of the house.

"Come here, Lata," she said. "I'll help you up."

I hesitated. I didn't really want to go first, but Aunt

Charlotte was anxious, signaling to me, and I didn't want to disappoint her. She lifted me up by my waist and I clambered over the ledge, then unlatched the door for her.

Inside, it was dark, empty and damp. The wide plank floor stretched from the door until it met the curled edge of an ancient sheet of stained linoleum that defined the kitchen area. A wood stove straddled the edge. Aunt Charlotte went to the stove and opened the little door. It swung crooked on one rusted hinge. She reached inside and fingered the ashes left from some long-ago fire.

"Aunt Marie always kept this burning to simmer her herbs," Aunt Charlotte said. She swung the door shut. The ashes left little black ovals on the tips of her gloved fingers. "Let me show you the upstairs."

She led me to a steep, narrow staircase. I felt my way up with my feet, clinging to the rail, watching the backs of her shoes through the faint light, her footing sure as it was on the steps of her own house. At the top of the steps was a small, narrow room with a peaked ceiling and walls grey with dirt and age. Sunlight poured in through a small window at the end of the room. Outside the window, I could see a bank of trees and behind them, a river.

"Aunt Marie used to do the wash in that river," Aunt Charlotte said. "She'd hang a clothesline between those two trees." She turned and stooped down. "Here's the closet from your dream," she said, pulling on a crude door just about my height that led to the eaves of the house. I nodded, even though the closet in my dream had a full-size door.

"Why don't you take a look inside?" She handed me a small flashlight, which hung from her car keys. "Don't

think about anything but your dream."

I flicked on the flashlight and shone it into the closet. The thin beam slid along the wall, catching on cobwebs and nests of old dust. The light snagged on something crudely carved into the wooden beams that formed the roof. The carving was in the lowest part of the closet, and I had to crawl to get to it. I laid on my belly and looked closely at the three images. One was a butterfly, the second a hummingbird, and the third was an owl. Underneath the owl was a sun and the word "Wabeno." I traced the carvings with my finger. Something about them seemed ancient, older than the house itself.

I called to Aunt Charlotte to come and see what I'd found. No answer. I scrambled from the closet and walked the length of the room, all the while telling myself this was part of a game and at any moment she'd jump out with a laugh, and then we'd go home.

"Aunt Charlotte?" I called down the steps. Only the creaks and groans of the old house replied.

I went down the stairs, gripping the handrail. I could see from the base of the steps that she was not there, but I circled the two rooms just the same, opening the rusted metal cabinet by the sink as though she would have climbed up and hidden in there. I paused at the window next to the door and peered out. The wind had picked up and the tall grass moved in waves like a golden lake. A hummingbird rose from its center and flew straight up, then disappeared behind the house. There was no sign of Aunt Charlotte.

The wind was rattling the windows, so I went back

upstairs to wait. It was sunnier there and not so damp. Aunt Charlotte would not be gone long, I told myself. I rattled her keys, and this reassured me — she couldn't have driven anywhere. She probably walked down to the river. I knelt in the sunlit window to watch her approach. The wind lifted dried leaves along the riverbank, settling them softly like bits of cloth. I thought I saw a woman running along the river, a cloud of silver hair behind her.

And then I saw the barbeque grill from my dream, large as a city lot, burning tall and hot until everything turned to ash. From the ash sprung pine cones that grew into a grove of trees where Uncle Jesse lay in a hammock. A hummingbird darted over him with a tobacco pouch hanging from her beak. She dropped a single leaf of tobacco, lit golden in the sun. It landed on his chest and burst into flames that bloomed into a cloud of orange butterflies. All around him, pine cones sprouted into a huge variety of trees, until the whole earth was covered with forest.

An owl landed in the poplar just outside the window. The branch sunk under its weight. The bird turned its head, looked right at me through the window and said, "Char. Lot." Then it flew away.

I turned to face the steps so I could watch for Aunt Charlotte. Almost immediately I felt someone—some human presence—standing behind me. By the time I turned back, it was gone. Then it started to tease me, coming so close that I'd almost feel it breathe on my neck, but really it was just a draft from the window. If Aunt Charlotte had been there, we could have ignored it together. Without her, every creak and jitter in the house,

every gust of wind against the window, could have been her, come back for me. Or it could have been Aunt Marie coming in with the sheets to make up a bed, or stirring a fire in the stove downstairs.

I sat there long enough for a rectangle of sunlight to move to my left and up the wall. Then I decided to sit at the top of the steps where I'd be sure to hear when Aunt Charlotte came back. And there I sat, looking down the dim staircase. From the corner of my eye I'd catch a glimpse of her hands in their dirty white prom gloves reaching for me, but it was a trick of the light.

Finally, those gloves really did reach for me. She was kneeling beside me, running her hands through my hair. I was angry that she'd left me there and now came back without explanation, but my relief was greater than my anger. I clung to her and said nothing, afraid that she'd take her hands away, that she'd stop looking at me so intently with her sorrowful, tender eyes, and I'd once again be alone.

"Did you see Aunt Marie?" she asked.

I shook my head. "I felt her, though, moving around the house. And I saw a woman with silver hair running along the river." I told her about the fire and Uncle Jesse in the hammock, the butterflies and the owl that said her name. I said all this to please her — to keep her interested in me.

"What does Wabeno mean?" I asked.

Aunt Charlotte's eyes went bright. She gathered me up against her chest and stroked my hair. She smelled like the dampness of earth. "I don't know much about it," she said. "All I know is they use fire for healing. They can't be

burned. Aunt Marie might have told me more when I got older."

She looked intently into the dark stairwell, as though she were seeing something that I couldn't see. "Your Uncle Jesse is a good man," she said with a distant quality in her voice that frightened me. "His obsession with that house is destroying him."

Aunt Charlotte paused to brush a piece of hair from my eyes. She seemed to be groping for words. Then she said, "You know how birds are born, right?"

"They come out of eggs," I said.

"What happens to the egg when the bird comes out?"

"It breaks open."

"If the bird were careful, could it keep the egg from breaking?"

"No."

"The egg has to break for the bird to be born, right?"

I nodded.

"Lata," Aunt Charlotte said, gripping my hands. "I am the egg, you are the bird."

WE CLUNG TO EACH OTHER as we walked back to the car, like refugees, pockets filled with the cones we had gathered from an old cedar tree. The sun had sunk low and the sky was streaked with a garish orange that settled on the remaining rain clouds. Aunt Charlotte had filled the back of the car with bags full of pine cones, clumps of sweet grass and mullein, yarrow and milkweed, along with a variety of tree saplings that were barely more than sticks, their roots covered in damp soil and wrapped in newspaper.

We were silent in the car, listening to the buzz of the fan. The setting sun made the rabbit's foot glow and it looked as though it might be warm to the touch. I took it from the rearview mirror and rubbed it lightly against my palm until I fell asleep. I slept for a long time, a sleep so deep and black that I could have been underground. I woke when Aunt Charlotte stopped at Earl & Sons Gas Food. By then my head was pounding from hunger. Aunt Charlotte bought a tin of aspirin and a bottle of apple juice for me. She also bought eight boxes of white taper candles and a red gasoline can, which she filled at the pump.

When we got back to the house, Uncle Jesse's van was not in the drive. The streetlights were out, and the house stood like a shadow on a wall. It might not have been there at all. But then we were on the porch, Aunt Charlotte had the key in the lock, and warm air was greeting us in the hallway. We squirmed out of our raincoats and left them in a heap by the front door. Aunt Charlotte stowed the can of gasoline in the back of the hall closet. Then she retrieved the paper bag from Earl & Sons.

"Let's get some light in this place," she said. She opened a box of candles and spilled them onto the doormat, then went to the kitchen for a matchbook. She lit one of the candles, dripped a pool of wax on the hall floor, stood another candle in the pool, and then lit that candle with the one in her hand. All down the hall she did this, going around the tarp in the corner where Uncle Jesse had left his plastering supplies, and ending with three candles on top of the banister. She did this with a zeal that I'd never seen in her before. The walls glowed like warm skin and it seemed to me that if I pressed my cheek against them they would be soft as Aunt Charlotte's belly.

When she had lit the last candle, Aunt Charlotte walked softly between them and pulled me up by my hands. We swayed together like smoke between the candles, light and grey as sparrows. I heard a melody so far off and faint that it might have only been a memory. And then I heard the scrape of Uncle Jesse's boots on the jute mat. Those boots were dangerous. They couldn't walk between candles, and when he opened the door and stepped into the hall, I saw the flames shudder like flowers on their stems.

"Christ, Charlotte, you'll burn the house down," Uncle Jesse said. He stood still, perhaps aware as I was of the danger of his boots, and looked at Aunt Charlotte. I looked at her too. The candlelight made her seem lit from within. A truck went by and a shiver ran through the floor that made the candles quiver. One fell and burned itself out. Uncle Jesse took a deep breath, as if that would stabilize the floor, then he crouched down and blew out a candle. One and then another. When he got to the dining room, he grabbed two silver egg cups from the cabinet and snuffed the candles two at a time. Aunt Charlotte and I stood still and watched. When he had snuffed out the last candle, he flicked on the hall switch and a harsh light flooded the room. Aunt Charlotte looked pale and small in this light. I touched her hand. It felt ice cold.

"Go up to bed, Lata," Uncle Jesse said, but he was looking at Aunt Charlotte.

I started up the steps, but then stopped to watch as he put his arms around her. When he stroked her back, her

body stiffened. The hall light fell hard on her cheek and I could see that he was no comfort.

THE NEXT MORNING, I woke up to Aunt Charlotte sitting on the edge of the bed, stroking my hair, smelling of damp earth. She was still dressed in her green t-shirt and jeans from the day before and I could tell she had already been in the yard, planting what she had gathered yesterday from near the farmhouse.

"For your birthday, sweetheart," she said, "a little early." She laid a package on my belly. I sat up and tore it open. Inside was a dark red dress with black and white triangles embroidered around the collar and sleeves. Aunt Charlotte helped me take off my pajama top and pull the dress over my head. I stood on the bed and spun around to model it for her.

"You look like a priestess," she said, smoothing my hair. "Now go brush your teeth and then come down to the sunroom. I have another present for you."

I got ready fast, anxious to see what else Aunt Charlotte had for me. As I came down the stairs, I could see that all of the candles from the night before were heaped in a pile next to Uncle Jesse's tarp. Remnants of the wax pools that had held them upright still lined the hallway. From the foot of the steps, I could see Aunt Charlotte pacing in the sunroom the way she sometimes did in the garden. The air around her was almost visible. It sparked with the things that were about to happen.

On the sunroom floor, Aunt Charlotte had a single white candle burning in a clay holder. Beside it was a small package wrapped in red cloth and tied with a yellow cord. She took my face in her hands and kissed my forehead, then led me to the candle.

"I want to show you something," she said. She moved her hand slowly, back and forth over the flame, then showed me her palm. It had a pink blush, as though the fire had caused her blood to run red again.

"The fire can't hurt me," she said. She lifted the candle and moved the flame over her cheeks. The heat made her skin glow. She looked healthier than she had all summer.

"It seems to be good for you," I said. Aunt Charlotte laughed and put the candle back on the floor.

"Yes, baby, the fire is good for me." She grabbed both of my hands, delighted, as though I'd said something funny or profound. Then she handed me the little package.

I don't know quite how to explain the feeling I had when the red cloth fell away and revealed the tobacco pouch that in my dream, I had pulled from the fire and slipped into my pocket. The leather was supple and worn, with a rich, complex smell.

"Aunt Marie gave me this pouch," she said. "I was just a little older than you. She showed me how to use it to offer something back to the earth for giving us so much, like we do in the garden. Now it's your turn."

She drew me close to her. I leaned into her chest, clutching the pouch, suddenly weak and heavy. "I have to go away," she said softly, "Like in your dream. That's why I gave you the pouch."

I felt a tightening in my chest. It got so tight that I couldn't breathe. Aunt Charlotte rocked me back and

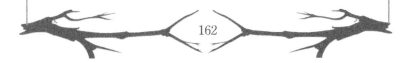

forth, whispered to me: No, I couldn't go with her. My first dream said I had to stay and have a picnic in the forest with Uncle Jesse. I'd know when the time came. Until then, I had to go home and listen close to my dreams. I could do it. All the dreams said I could do it. She had to go. I had to stay. Everything would be all right.

13

INTO THE FIRE

Charlotte

I GO INTO THE HALLWAY, scattering a paper bag full of pine cones that I gathered from Aunt Marie's house yesterday. These ones need fire to open. I can see my suitcase near the back door. I climb the stairs in my bare feet, gasoline can in one hand, box of wooden matches in the other. I scatter pine cones across the upstairs hallway, then open the door that leads to the attic stairs. There's a weird smell. The steps feel kind of tacky. Why did he varnish the attic stairs? He can be so obsessive.

I reach the top of the staircase and step into the attic. Everything is going just right. I can see outside the window. It's early, just before dawn. The sky and the treetops are still in shadow, but I can still see Lata standing there with her suitcase, holding the tobacco pouch in her hand, stroking it with her thumb. She's so trusting. I couldn't do this if she wasn't so trusting.

I push the boxes of clothes under the eaves, each with a splash from the gas can, and throw a match into the first one. An explosion of light. Beautiful. The clothes are burning fast with the gasoline. It's a little bit scary. I step back a few feet from where it's burning. Seems the roof is already starting to catch. I pour a line of gasoline on the floor as I walk toward the steps. There's a sudden spark come off the clothes and I jump back, spilling a pool of gasoline on the floor right near the open door. Another spark jumps and the line of gasoline turns into fire. A flash. The entire staircase is in flames.

Oh my God.

It must be the varnish. He's put it on all the floors except the sunroom. That means all the floors in the house are burning.

I move back toward the window, the only place that makes sense. I'll climb out somehow, though it doesn't seem possible. I rattle the window, struggling to push it up, then look out as though someone would be there to help me. And there is Lata, standing in the first light of dawn, looking down at the tobacco pouch in her hand, her face placid, trusting.

No Lata. Don't look up!

She can't see me panic. If she sees me panic it's all over. All of her trust will be broken and she'll be traumatized. How could I be so stupid? I can't let her see me panic.

I watch Lata's eyes move up toward the window. Fire raging. Heat on my back. She's looking right at me.

A sudden calm. Time slowing down. I'm filling myself with so much love for her. The love is knocking out all the fear. I'm waving at her. Waving and smiling and loving her. She's waving back.

She's holding that pouch with so much trust. Why is it so flat? I forgot to fill it with tobacco for her. How will she remember to make offerings? If she doesn't remember to make offerings, she'll be so alone with all she can see.

Her life will be hard.

I have to do it. I have to offer myself. There's no other way. I'm using everything I've got to will a piece of my soul down into that pouch, so Lata won't be alone.

Everything goes white.

When the world comes back, Lata's hand is in mine. I'm holding her hand, so now I have the strength to do it — to disappear. They can't find anything left of me. That's the only way Lata will know I survived. The sooner my body starts burning, the more likely there'll be nothing left. And if there is, the spirits will take care of it.

I'm turning toward the fire. Everything is so slow. I can take my sweet time.

The wing of an owl. A flash of fear.

Turning toward my death. Feeling Lata's hand as mine and spilling over with love for her, turning, turning, so much love, and there's no fire — just the open arms of a blinding light.

I run to my love — moth to flame.

Part TWO

ON THE LAST DAY OF THE WORLD
I WOULD WANT TO PLANT A TREE.
                                    –WS MERWYN

14

LETTERS FROM THE DENSE WORLD

Jesse

TUES / 9 AM / VIA EMAIL

Good morning Lata,
Welcome back to Hermitage Street. When did you arrive?
It's been more than 40 years since I last saw you. I'm surprised to hear that you are there now, though of course, it makes sense that you would want to visit one last time, given the tragedy of the fire you witnessed so long ago.

I heard from the real estate broker that you stopped the workers who came to cut open the fence to bring the bulldozer in. You told one of them your name was Charlotte and the other that your name was Lata, but I know it must be Lata because of course, Charlotte is dead. No one else besides Lata and Charlotte know who is listed in the trust, other than my lawyer (and my Uncle Roy, but he's in a nursing home, so it can't have anything to do with him). So, Lata, I'm writing to reassure you that I have no intention of leaving you out of this deal. My lawyer already wrote to you via your mother, and she told us that you have received the letter asking for your notarized signature. It's okay that we haven't yet received the signature, as according to your mother, you are in some remote part of Asia and such things can take longer to get done there. We are happy to wait for the paperwork, but we're on a deadline to close this deal and so we have to get the work started so the inspector can get in.

I know this property may have sentimental value for you. Given this, I understand why you might want to wait on the work. I presume it has been a long time since you've been there? I haven't been there since the day the house burned. I long ago moved on from that house and all that went on there, as I'm not one to wallow in the past, and since the property was in a declining neighborhood and had nothing but rubble on it, it wasn't worth the trouble to sell it until now.

Let me make it clear that the way my Uncle Roy set up the trust, you are named as Charlotte's heir, and her half does not revert to me in the event of Charlotte's death. This was, frankly, a clerical error, but I assure you I will not contest it. I am more than willing to honor the trust as it was written. And just in case you didn't get the original letter from my lawyer but only heard about it from your mother, I'll say again what the situation is.

I have an offer on the property from the tech company that moved into the old candy factory on Ravenswood Street. Because it is such a large lot, it is extremely valuable to them. The prices in the neighborhood have soared in the last five years since so many tech professionals have moved there, and the whole area is being revived. Their offer is phenomenal, well over a million. Just as the trust says, whether it's Charlotte (which of course, is impossi-

ble), or Lata, you will get half, which will come to at least $500,000 after lawyer fees — and likely more, as we are still in negotiations.

I am traveling at the moment and anyway don't live in the area, so it is not possible for me to come personally to the property and meet you there as you requested when you stopped the workers. I hope this letter will suffice in place of that, and you will allow the workers to do what they were hired to do when they come tomorrow morning. Rest assured, it is in all of our interest. Though it has been a long time since I've seen you, I am happy that this deal will set you up in your old age.

Lata, I tried to get your cell number from your mother, but she doesn't have one for you. Please text me at 600-444-5398 so that I know you received this.

Sincerely,
Jesse Martin

TUES / 2 PM / VIA EMAIL AND COURIER

Dear Lata,
Since you again stopped the workers with the same request that I come to the property, I can only assume you didn't receive my email of this morning and so I am sending it again via my broker's courier. Please understand that my only interest is in selling the property — cleaning up what has been left unsettled all these years. I have no

interest in revisiting it and meeting you there for any reason whatsoever. Once the deal is completed, I am happy to meet and treat you to a celebration dinner.

Sincerely,

Your Uncle Jesse

Dear Lata (Charlotte?),

Your mother tells me that you are still in Asia, so I don't know that this is you. But of course, it can't be Charlotte. I know they never found her remains, but they would have if they had persisted. Charlotte couldn't have gotten out of the house. All the inspectors said so.

Whoever it is, as I told you in previous letters, I am traveling and cannot come to the property. I have now paid the workers for a full day of bulldozing when nothing at all has been done. I don't want to have to do this again today. This is very expensive and only cuts into your share of the profit.

I still haven't heard from you personally — only through the workers. If there is something you want to discuss with me to get this going, please text or email me as soon as you receive this. I can send a taxi to take you to my lawyer's office any time today or tomorrow for a video conference with me, and I will rearrange my schedule to make this possible. This is the best I can offer, as I am not in the area.

Sincerely,

Jesse

Thurs / 9 am / via email and Courier

To whom it may concern:

Since I have not heard back from you about the video conference, but only received the same message again that you want me to come to the property, I have no choice but to take this step.

Lata's mother has told me that she has not arrived yet from Asia, and it is not possible that Charlotte is at the property, as she died more than 40 years ago in the fire. This means that whoever you are, you are not named in the trust.

Perhaps Lata sent you to keep watch until she arrives? If that is the case, I assume she has not received any of these letters. Given this, I have again emailed all of them to her. I will postpone the workers for another day as I await her reply. Meanwhile, I ask you to leave the property, and advise you that if the workers are again stopped tomorrow, I will have you arrested for trespassing.

Sincerely,

Jesse Martin

Dear Lata,

I know yesterday must have been terrible for you and I am so sorry to have put you through it. I honestly didn't think it would come to arrest. I really only meant to wake you up from this very frustrating lack of communication, but my real estate broker's office informed the workers of what I had written to you and they are the ones who called the police. I assure you it was not me.

I heard that you refused to show identification at the property, which was really the main thing we wanted — just to know who it is we're dealing with. I understand if you didn't have it with you — if it was at your hotel or something. Again, I didn't intend at all for you to be arrested, but when you were silent in response to their questions, I heard that they took you to the station and got this mugshot, which they sent to me so that I could identify you. I know they held you awaiting my reply, and I'm sorry it took me so long — I was in meetings all afternoon and didn't check my messages until late in the evening.

It was more than 40 years since I've seen you or Charlotte. Last we were together, you were an eight-year-old girl and Charlotte only 25, so I guess it's not surprising that I can't positively identify either of you from this photo. I told the police it was definitely one of you and to release you without charge, since I know it can't be Charlotte and I don't want you to have an arrest record.

I see from the side shot that you have a long dark braid — the same as Charlotte used to wear. I know that isn't exactly the fashion, especially for an American woman, so I can't help but wonder if you have been influenced by Charlotte all these years? After all, you spent quite a bit of time with her that summer, and it did end tragically. I'm sorry if I have been insensitive to any grief you may still be holding for her.

I know that the police were unhappy with you for being uncooperative and they were toying with charging you with resisting arrest. I hope that I was able to convince them otherwise. Please don't do anything that might get them involved again. I just want this to end well for all of us.

Now that I remember how this might be traumatic for you, please know that if I could come, I would. But I am in Europe, attending an award ceremony for a house I designed. I don't know if your mother told you, but I am an architect. The award is very prestigious and it is important that I stay here for all the events surrounding it. I hope you understand.

Your Aunt Charlotte would be happy to know that it is not a restored Victorian, but a cutting edge, high-end eco-design, and features sustainable lumber from of all places, the Menominee Tribe's lumber mill. Very lovely and rare yellow birch. So you see, she has influenced me as well. (I assume you remember that Charlotte was descended from the Menominee? Of course, that means you were as well.)

Anyway, you can see that I am not there for a good reason and I will ask them not to arrest you or do anything else that would upset you. But please help me with this, Lata. The money I will get in this sale is extremely important to me. Award or not, I have run into some issues and need this sale to go through smoothly. And from what your mother tells me, you have been living rather simply and have nothing saved for emergencies or for your retirement. Given this, please allow the work to begin and know that I will come and visit you in person just as soon as I am able.

With affection,

Your Uncle Jesse

ps. Do you not have a cell phone? I will have my broker leave one for you so that you have a way to get in touch with me in an emergency.

Mon / 8:00 AM / VIA EMAIL AND COURIER

Dear Lata,

I hope you weren't too frightened when the bulldozer came this morning. I know it was very early. I assumed that you would be okay with it, after my last letter, even though I didn't hear back from you. We were hoping to get it in before you arrived, to avoid any encounter that might attract the police in some way.

Please don't blame the workers. It was my idea to do it this way. I wasn't trying to trick you. I was trying to protect you from another encounter with the police. At that hour, I thought you would be asleep at your hotel. There was no way for us to know that you were inside the fence, on the property, since my broker says that the small gate I had originally installed is well padlocked, so there is no way to get

inside. But then the workers said that you had been inside before as well. Can you please tell me how you got in?

In any case, standing in front of the bulldozer the way you did was extremely dangerous. It was barely dawn and difficult for the driver to see, with all the shrubbery he had to get through. It's a miracle that he saw you and you weren't killed.

They say you haven't moved from that spot in front of the bulldozer since, and that the bulldozer is half inside the property, half outside. Lata, this is dangerous for you. The police are not going to allow it to stay like that, blocking the sidewalk. If I promise you that we won't do anything else, will you at least let them bring the bulldozer all the way in? Then we can close up the fence with a gate. But we can't do that with the bulldozer half in and half out, and I can't stop the police from intervening if someone on the block reports it, which they certainly will. So you see, this is for your protection, to keep you from getting arrested again. Remember, you've already annoyed the precinct sergeant. They won't take kindly to you if they bring you back there.

I've asked that the courier wait for your reply to this. But please don't wait for an exchange with me to move out of the way. Just let the bulldozer in and the whole drama will be over. We can put up the gate and it's done.

Please?

Uncle Jess

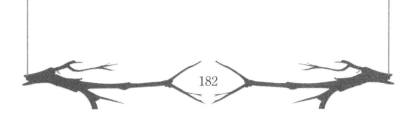

Dear Lata,

Of course you were right, that it was just as easy to back the bulldozer out as to bring it forward, but would bringing it forward really have damaged anything? I mean, it's a burned out house on an overgrown lot. So I paid to have a bulldozer towed there and back for no reason. And I will have to pay it again, because as you can see, that house needs to be removed. The rubble is dangerous. Someone fell through it once. That's why I had to put up the barbed wire.

Still, I can't tell you how relieved I was to hear that the bulldozer is now off the sidewalk, the gate is up, and we don't have to worry about another police encounter.

I'm also relieved because this is the first real indication I've gotten that you are receiving these letters. I was distressed when I heard from the courier that he has been leaving them stuck in the side gate, as he can't get inside and doesn't see you from the sidewalk. In fact, he says he hasn't seen you at all until yesterday, and so I'm not even certain you've gotten all my other letters. I've asked the real estate broker to put a lockbox on the gate so the courier can get in and give you my letters directly. I hope that isn't too disruptive for you, but I do need to know that you are receiving them.

It's hard for me to imagine that you are staying on the property. After all, there's no house there anymore. Did you set up a tent? I would still like to know how you get through the fence.

Please get in touch with me directly. I did send you a cell phone, remember?

Warmly,

Uncle Jesse

ps—the award ceremony went very well.

Dear Lata,

This is getting out of hand.

Did you add a second padlock to both gates? Because when the workers came this morning, they couldn't open the new gate, and so the broker came over to open the side gate, and that one had a second padlock as well.

You wouldn't be able to tell necessarily from these letters, but this situation is extremely stressful for me. I know I must be writing to Lata. I know that Charlotte is dead. But you are inside and then outside of a six-foot fence topped with barbed wire, again and again. Your mother keeps telling me you're not even back from Asia yet. I can't tell if you're here and not telling her, or if I'm actually writing to Charlotte, that somehow she survived the fire and has been staying there all along. Is that possible? That can't be possible. And then I think that maybe both are happening. Maybe Charlotte is inside and you are outside and that's why this is so baffling. Or maybe they just think they see Charlotte. Can you see? This is driving me crazy.

I'm having all these weird dreams. I can't sleep through the night. The deadline is creeping up for the sale, and I have all these things I'm supposed to have done by then. I haven't received your signature and the lawyer keeps calling me. If I don't get this money soon, I'm going to be sued because I'm short the equivalent of one yellow birch tree. One miscalculation, and there's not enough wood. The Menominee lumber mill says they can't cut any more yellow birch for some reason—not even one goddam tree—and I already bought all the yellow birch they had.

But then I've got this impossible client who says if all the lumber doesn't match, the commission is off. Even though I just won this award for it, she'll use my design, which she already paid for, but null my contract to oversee the building. Do you have any idea what that will do to my reputation right on the heels of this award? Not to mention that I already bought all these expensive materials. I've got to get my hands on a load of sustainable yellow birch that matches what I have as soon as possible, and to make that happen, I need to find someone to pay off with a wad of cash that I will get from the sale of this property or I'll be bankrupt. Because of one fucking tree.

Lata, or Charlotte, or whoever the hell you are, I can't take this anymore. Every time they actually get to see you, you say the same thing — "tell him to meet me here." Nothing else. That's all you say. Can't you be a little flexible? Where's your empathy, for God's sake? Just, please, let the workers back onto the property and let the bulldozer do its job so this sale can go through. Why are you making this so hard?

I don't even know if you'll get this. I don't even know if you're getting any of these letters. I don't even know why I'm writing this.

Jesse

ps. If all you're going to say is "Tell him to meet me here," don't even bother.

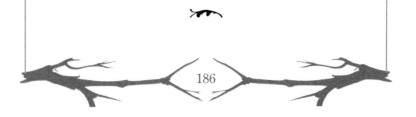

Tues / 11:30 AM / VIA EMAIL AND COURIER

Dear Lata or Charlotte, or both of you,
What do you mean, "Tell him to come and I will give him a yellow birch tree?" Are you toying with me? What the hell. I'm in this big mess that I already confessed to you, which was probably a huge mistake, and now you're telling me that you can give me a yellow birch tree? That's the most ridiculous thing I ever heard.

If this is some kind of revenge, it's working.

Jesse

ps. After the sale of the property falls through, maybe you and my eco-chic client can get together and figure out what you want to do with all the sustainable yellow birch I bought for her project. Hey, maybe you can give her the yellow birch tree.

Dear whoever,

The broker sent me a photo of the piece of bark you gave her, and yes, I see that it is yellow birch, but I don't see how you have that there on the property. It makes no sense at all. It's just a burned out house with an overgrown yard.

What I find stunning is that I'm trying to clear this property so that I can give YOU half a million dollars. Most people would be cooperative in a situation like this. But you want me to fly back from Europe rather than pick up a goddam cell phone.

Another day the workers couldn't work. Now I've paid for six days, plus a bulldozer tow. It's getting to the point where I'm going to have to come there, but I'm warning you, it's not going to feel like a family reunion.

Jesse

ps. The courier costs a fortune. Use the goddam cell phone.

WED / 9AM / VIA EMAIL AND COURIER

Dear Lata and friends,

Now what are you up to? I just got a call from my broker. She said little girls are going door to door in the area offering people milkweed to put in their yards. They say it's for the monarch butterflies that are on the way, and it comes from "the butterfly forest" — my goddam property.

So the workers are out because of butterflies now? Since when is the burned out house a butterfly resort? I don't know what you're up to, but I sure would like to understand what this is all about.

Jesse

THURS / 11:30 AM / VIA EMAIL AND COURIER

Dear Lata,
So I don't know if this will help or hurt us in negotiations, but I heard from my broker that these butterflies are now the talk of the neighborhood. She says they're coming in small flocks now and people can see them going into the property. Some of the people who took the milkweed from your little elves have butterflies in their yards, too, so now everyone at the tech company wants some milkweed.

That's all very sweet, but please don't get any ideas about opening up the gate and letting anyone in to see the butterflies. If you'd let the bulldozer in six days ago, that might have been possible, but there's a big liability there. That house is dangerous. YOU shouldn't even be there. So don't do it.

I've given up on the idea that you will be reasonable with me, so the workers won't be back until I get there. I'll let you know when I get my flight booked. Meanwhile keep the gate locked. And have that yellow birch ready for me, okay? Preferably cut and planed.

Jesse

15

HIDDEN

EYES

Jesse

IN THE YEARS SINCE THE FIRE, I've carried two pictures in my mind of the house on Hermitage Street. In one, the lawn is bright green and neatly mowed, stretching from the picket fence to the climbing rose bushes that twist elegantly up the porch rails in full maturity, spilling large, trailing blooms in a blushing pink. I can see blue sky and sun reflected in the upper window of the turret, and the peaked roof with its dormers still fully intact — including the one where Charlotte was last seen waving, unmoved by the wall of fire behind her. The house gleams with a perfection that has become real to me since it has held this form in my mind more than 40 years now, unchanged.

There is another, darker picture that I've carried alongside this perfect version. Where once the house stood, there is only a pile of blackened rubble, still with that sour smell of scorched wood. The rubble is completely surrounded by brambles heavy with thorns, since the hybrid roses Charlotte so vehemently opposed went feral, crowding out all else, but refusing to bloom. The oak tree has split and one side has fallen, its branches dead and bare. Surrounding this apocalypse is the six-foot, chain-link fence I had installed at the behest of the neighborhood precinct captain soon after the fire to keep out the children and bums. Atop that fence, circles of barbed wire guarantee it will be left alone.

When I arrived early in the morning at the corner of Sunnyside and Hermitage, I was surprised to see neither of these pictures, and for a minute, was tempted to double check the address. From where I stood on the sidewalk in front of what would have been the walkway to the front door, I could see on the other side of the chain-link fence only a massive tangle of green, gold and red vegetation so thick, there was no way for me to tell if there was anything at all left of the old Victorian. The wide canopy of the oak spread overhead, along with the tops of trees I'd never seen before. Though I couldn't see any birds, I knew there were many given the overlapping symphony of their morning songs.

The street, I barely recognized. Many of the houses — including Mrs. Petty's — had been razed to make way for chic townhouses to shelter those who came to work for the tech company now lodged in the old candy factory the next block over. They had their own stop on the newly routed commuter train that ran behind the factory lofts where the freight trains used to go. Nano Square, they called it, and it was lined with gourmet coffee shops. I stopped in one on the way over—excellent cold-press coffee and free hi-speed with ample charging stations. Nothing else was open yet, but I passed a couple of eco-chic clothing boutiques, an upscale wireless accessory shop and a foodie market that had a sign for artisan cheeses and organic, slow-food carry out, where I thought I'd stop for lunch.

All of this boded well for the sale of the property, and yet, walking along the fence, avoiding a puddle in order to protect the Italian leather shoes I bought before I left Europe, I was struck with a sense of foreboding. Nothing was as I thought it would be. I kept looking for a spot where I might glimpse something familiar through the dense foliage, but none of it yielded. Finally, I saw up ahead the place where I had advised the workers to put in the new gate. Surely, something known would be visible from there.

Peering through that gate, I could see where the bull-dozer had flattened the thick wall of shrubs — at least as far as the spot where Lata must have seated herself for hours, refusing to budge until the bulldozer backed out. The shrubbery there was not as tall and of a different character. I can't say that I knew what it was, but there were clusters of red blooms that I found appealing, and a hum-mingbird hovered nearby. Beyond those bushes, there was a stand of pines.

I was shocked at the maturity of those trees. Could they really be the sticks that Charlotte stuck in the ground in a pattern that seemed altogether random? The whole thing was so disorienting. I couldn't even tell where the house ought to be. I looked up to find the canopy of the oak and angled myself toward it, hoping to catch a glimpse of whatever was left of the house, but there was nothing discernible. I moved my head about, cheek against the chain-links, trying to find a hole in the foliage that I could see through until I banged my forehead on something heavy: A strange padlock engraved with what appeared to be a lion. It was old and heavy, carefully cast and weathered a grey-green. Everything about it seemed ancient. Lata must have brought it back from somewhere in Asia, but still, it was unnerving to see it there, hanging alongside the standard silver padlock and chain that the workers had installed.

I felt someone near and looked around, but I was alone on the street. Still, there were eyes on me.

"Hello?" I called into the foliage.

Silence.

"Lata, are you there? It's Jesse. I'm at the gate."

I bent forward in an awkward posture, listening. No sound. But then I saw a flash of movement. I'd know that walk anywhere, the swing of that braid. Charlotte. I felt heat rise, my intestines go loose. This couldn't be. It's easy to imagine things, peering through foliage, especially when you're tired and jetlagged. She was there and gone in such a flash.

I heard a rustle.

"Lata?"

Snap of a twig.

The click of footsteps on the sidewalk and I swung my head around. A well-dressed woman walked by, holding the turquoise leash of a fluffy white dog. I must have looked ridiculous to her in my fine Italian wool, a man near retirement age bent over, peering into an empty lot. I stood up straight and turned toward the street, took a sip of my coffee, but all the while I felt those hidden eyes.

Enough of this. I walked purposely to the end of the block around to where the side gate should have been and almost passed by it, what with all the overgrown shrubs poking out through the chain-links, obscuring the fence. Someone had roughly trimmed the area around the gate, which gave the impression of a lopsided entrance to an old English garden. My broker must have had this done — perhaps when she had the lockbox installed. The gate was as far as they got with that tunnel. On the other side, there was a massive tangle of shrubs with only a barely discernible footpath, the bramble of sharp branches around it so thick, you'd need a machete to walk it.

Again, I found two padlocks securing the gate: The one I bought more than 40 years ago, now rusted with age, and another ancient-looking one made of heavy iron, this with a carving of a dragon breathing fire. I own this place, for God's sake, I wanted to say to that padlock, to those ghostly eyes still watching me like a predator. I strained over the fence to peer through the shrubbery, calling loudly for Lata, but only the silent rustle of leaves, the cackle of a crow.

I leaned my forehead on the fence post, unsure what to do. My eyes landed on a bit of wood tangled in the shrubbery — a remnant of the white picket fence that used to circle the front yard. A sudden gloom came over me, standing there at the side gate, a chill going into my bones, my Italian wool too thin for the morning air. I had prepared to feel irritation, perhaps indifference or a tinge of nostalgia — even a haunting. But the sadness I felt looking at that length of fence twisted in the shrubbery — I didn't prepare for that.

I never thought I would come here again. Why would I? The fire happened so long ago, this abandoned lot the only remains of a youthful dream: that I would make a place in the world, prove something to my Uncle Roy, my dead mother — prove that I could provide in a way that my father had not. I would give the ordinary to a woman and child — those things deemed valuable by voices that seemed to come out of the buildings and cars, murmur in the display windows of the shops. Never mind my own appetites — the darkness of them, the exultation. All of it I would force into this project, this one chance given me by my Uncle Roy, benevolent king—the one on top who knew what was what. The hapless, disadvantaged son of my mother's misstep — that was the "me" who last saw Lata on the front lawn of this house, last saw Charlotte asleep in her hammock surrounded by those newly planted sticks, not long before she lit the match that turned this dream to ash.

Now I could see nothing of the house where once I sawed and painted with great zeal, imagining tinkling wine glasses in the restored dining room, a fire in the fieldstone fireplace keeping the cold and the chaos at bay. And Charlotte, transformed into a charming hostess, hair loose and brushed to a sheen, wearing the dress she wore the day of our wedding with the elegant white gloves that stretched to her elbows, her eyes filled with laughter instead of the eerie vastness I remembered. I thought she would get over that cedar being cut, that stretch of forest being removed. Yes it was a beautiful old tree, but there are others. And this is a city, after all.

The wind picked up with sudden force, rattling the newly budding leaves. A shiver went through my body and I could feel those hidden eyes on me—the eyes of the forest. Charlotte's eyes. It took all I had to push away the sense of haunting so that I could remember the lure of a cheerful café near the train stop. Through the window, I had seen a pile of fresh scones and inviting, overstuffed chairs. I turned and walked briskly in their direction.

Soon, I was sitting in one of those chairs, warmed by the softness of its velvety fabric, breathing in the aroma of fresh bakery, my hands wrapped around a mug of cappuccino with foam thick and creamy—just the way I like it. A pleasant din of conversation hummed in the background. Emboldened by these comforts, I brushed away the crumbs from my lemon scone, opened my laptop and composed an email to Lata:

SEPT 12 / 7:50 AM / VIA COURIER AND EMAIL

Good morning, Lata,
I arrived from Europe early this morning and immediately came to see you at the property, but since you put padlocks on both gates, there was no way for me to get in. I called for you, but you didn't hear me—or maybe you were at your hotel.

Since you weren't there, I went to the Aroma Café on Ravenswood Street. I am here now, so please come over. You'll find me in the back corner near the window. If you can't get here by 11am, then please let me know a good time for us to meet. They have great lemon scones — my treat.
Uncle Jesse

Writing such a normal letter relieved the sense of haunting considerably. I copied it to my broker with a request that she have it sent by courier, then leaned back in my chair and looked out the window. A misty drizzle softened the edges of things as fashionable commuters rushed by in a blur of color under black umbrellas. The hypnotic quality was amplified by the café's music, which had changed to what seemed to be a soundtrack from a sci-fi movie, and my eyelids went heavy until I started to doze, the din of voices and rattle of silverware comforting as the sounds of home.

I'm not sure how much time had passed when I felt a hand on my arm, small and light. I blinked open my eyes. There stood a girl of about 10. A bright green raincoat was buttoned up to her neck, the collar turned up, so that her face seemed in that moment like a flower on its stem. Tiny drops of water covered her spray of dark hair and sparkled like diamonds under the overhead lights. The steadiness of her eyes, so clear and sure, startled me, half-dreaming as I was. She greeted me with solemn formality.

"Are you Uncle Jesse?" she asked, and I nodded, a bit taken aback by the "uncle" part. "I'm Millie."

"Nobody's named Millie anymore," I said. "Where'd you get such an old-fashioned name?"

"It's just my name, same like my grandma."

She held up a pair of weathered, old work boots. They looked strangely familiar.

"These will be much better for you in the rain. Save your fancy shoes."

"That's nice of you, Millie. What makes you think

197

they'll fit?"

"Cause they're yours, that's why."

I took the boots from her and examined them. They were a bit musty but had been freshly cleaned and conditioned — I could smell the saddle soap. Inside the back of the boots, my initials were written in black marker, just as I had done when I used to work for Kroemer at their construction sites back when I was 19.

"Where did you get these?" I asked.

"Just put them on," Millie ordered like a stern fairy godmother, the diamonds sparkling in her hair.

As though enchanted, I did as I was told. They were a bit stiff but fit surprisingly well. As soon as I started to lace them, I knew without a doubt they had been mine — a relic from a past life. It'd been a long time since I'd worn work boots, seeing as I had climbed the ladder, become the architect—the boss. I felt a wave of nostalgia.

Millie put my Italian leather shoes in a grocery bag, then stood with arms folded across her chest. "Put your laptop away and let's go," she said.

I zipped my laptop case and reluctantly gave up my seat. The cafe was full. No way would I get this seat back.

I KEPT WATCHING MY FEET move in those boots — the same feet that belonged to the 19-year-old who met Charlotte at an old cedar tree on Kroemer's construction site. How strange, to wear those same boots as I followed Millie down Hermitage Street along the fence that held in the mass of foliage where the house used to be. A younger version of my feet now occupied those boots, and I could

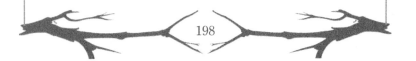

feel something of his sensibility rising up into the rest of me, coloring my inclinations. The rain had turned into a mist, for which I was grateful, seeing as I had left my raincoat hanging on the back of a chair in the airport, and I took pleasure in the fine spray of cool air.

When we reached the side gate, Millie took a large key from her pocket and opened the dragon padlock. The chain rattled as she slid it off the gate. "You'll have to get the other lock," she said.

I dug for my keys. There was one in the lockbox, but all those years, I'd kept the original on my keychain. The old lock was so rusted, I had to struggle to get it to turn.

"How do you normally get in?" I asked.

"We have a hidden passageway," Millie said, "but don't worry, it's hard to find. And you have to be small to get through."

The lock creaked open and Millie pushed open the gate as though I were the guest and she the owner. If anyone else had done that I would have been annoyed, but something about the formality of her serious little face made me smile, and I followed her lead down a narrow path cut between the brambles of shrubbery. The morning sun shone through the leaves of the trees, and the air had a moist, fresh scent.

It had been a while since I'd walked in anything resembling a forest. Over the years as I gained more success, my life had become hectic and civilized. Even though I specialized in designing eco-buildings, lately I lived largely in cafés and meeting rooms, the best of which had a view of a garden from the window. It felt a little foreign to walk on packed earth. I enjoyed the sensuality of it and I have to admit, I was glad to be wearing the work boots. I liked not having to worry about my shoes.

"Here we are," she said, gesturing toward a sweep of greenery, low to the ground. "They like the milkweed, but you'll see more if you look up."

"More what?"

"Butterflies." She was clearly annoyed. "See? They're all over the cedars."

And sure enough, they were. There were hundreds of them — maybe thousands. I couldn't tell, because with orange wings folded and flattened, they looked like bright leaves. I turned toward Millie, who was crouched in a patch of orange jewelweed gently extending her hand to a butterfly. It alighted on her finger. The sweat from my palm made the handle of my leather briefcase feel slick. Something in me didn't want to take any of it in.

"I came to see Lata," I said. "Do you know where she is?"

As I spoke, Millie's butterfly fluttered away and she put her hands on her hips. "Uncle Jesse. Did you know these butterflies have been disappearing? Can't you see how special this is?"

"Very special, Millie," I said. "Now where's Lata?"

Millie rolled her eyes. "Follow me."

16

RELUCTANT

GURU

Jesse

SHE WAS A RELUCTANT GURU on the porch of a ruined house. She had maybe four disciples. She wouldn't have called them that — would have been horrified at the word. Nor would she have called herself a guru. But I felt it from the first — the rock of her, something sunk in deep that only bobbed and floated in me like a nervous fish.

I had meant to take charge, turn on the charm, get her to sign within the hour and then take her to lunch. But nothing had prepared me for the sight of her standing on what was left of the front porch, bending over a pile of old newspapers that four little girls were folding like origami into small cups. The deliberateness of her movements as she flicked her braid over her shoulder, the way she adjusted the old tobacco pouch that dangled from a leather belt slung low on her hip — it was all so familiar. She turned then and looked at me, placid eyes filled with light. I was startled into a dream.

"You've hardly aged," I said. I was speaking to Charlotte.

She smiled. "But I was just a little girl the last time I saw you."

I was relieved to hear her identity confirmed as Lata, yet something in me saw only Charlotte. She stepped off the porch into the dappled sunlight.

"It must be strange for you to be here," she said. "It's been a long time." I could see, then, the fine lines around her eyes, strands of silver in her hair.

"We're ready for the milkweed," said Millie. Each of the girls had put six of the origami cups into little trays that had been made from thick layers of newspaper, and they stood in a row now, as though on display.

"Nice work," said Lata. "You're all getting the hang of it. Millie, how about you help the girls choose the milk-weed while I talk with Uncle Jesse?"

Millie nodded, and the girls followed her down the path, each holding their newspaper tray as though it were made of cut crystal.

"Quite an operation you've got here," I said, trying to bring myself back to the present.

"It just happened," she said, as though she had nothing to do with it.

You'd think we would have been more curious about each other, given it had been a lifetime since I'd last seen her standing right there as the house burned, when the forest was still lawn. But somehow, the facts of her life and all the questions I had for her seemed irrelevant as we sat down together on the porch steps and watched a progression of hummingbirds milk the red trumpet flowers that covered a nearby shrub. The forest held a freshness that wiped things clean, seeing as no one had been here to disturb it. The gloom I had experienced earlier vanished

like fog in a burst of sunlight, and I felt inexplicably happy.

Good to see the place one more time," I said, as I reached into my leather briefcase for the file that held the contract.

Lata put her hand on my arm. Her touch was strangely familiar. "You haven't seen the half of it yet. Let me give you a tour."

"I've seen the butterflies, if that's what you mean. Millie showed me on the way in," I said, thinking to move things along. Then I remembered. "But didn't you say something about yellow birch?"

Lata nodded and motioned for me to follow.

She led me past a stand of white pines into what used to be the backyard. That's when I first saw the sunroom where Charlotte had taken refuge — the only part of the house that hadn't been destroyed. The metal roof was still in place, and from this angle, it looked like a freestanding cottage. The oak tree was larger and more twisted than I remembered, and as we got closer, I saw that a hammock was strung from trunk to wall, the large window slid up high, just as Charlotte had kept it so she could use it like a door. I stopped on the path to look, time bending, the unfamiliar trees mixing with what had existed all those years only as memory and dream.

"The hammock was here when I came," said Lata. "Millie's older sister, Calla, put it there. The hooks were already in place. Do you want to see the inside?"

"No," I said with a sudden sharpness. "I've got a lot to get done today. Let's get to the birch."

Lata nodded and walked on, unperturbed by my

ill-humor. Her equanimity made me feel like a surly teen-
ager, but that couldn't stop the churning in my gut. How
was it that all I had worked for was destroyed, and only the
part Charlotte used was still here? That the sunroom had
a metal roof and shared a stone wall with the fireplace in
the adjoining dining room wasn't relevant to this question
— underneath, I felt singled out by fate. Watching the dark
braid swing down Lata's back as she led me along the
twisting path, I felt a bitter resentment. The venom of it
surprised me — I'd thought I'd gotten over it.

When we emerged from the pines, I saw the stand of
golden birch — the exact variety I had bought from the
Menominee — and in a flash I went from feeling crossed
by fate to utterly blessed. How impossible it seemed, that
the rare tree I needed desperately to save my reputation
— to save myself from bankruptcy — was right here, on
the property I owned. In a surge of gratitude and excitement, I brushed passed Lata to get a closer look. The birch
were on the small side — they are slow growers, and 40
years is really the minimum to make them worth
cutting — but there was one that was markedly thicker
than the others. I put my hands around the trunk to verify
the diameter, sense the width of the planks it would pro-
duce. It would work — I was sure of it.

"I can't believe it," I said to Lata, waves of relief moving through my body as the implications became clear.
"There really is a yellow birch."

Lata smiled. "Of course. You can take three. I'll show
you which ones."

"Don't bother," I said, feeling suddenly magnanimous.

"This is the only one I need."

"Not that one," said Lata. "It's the most established tree — the mother of this cluster. See how the ones to the left are crowded together? Take three from there, and the others will grow to full size. It will be helpful to the whole stand of trees for those three to be removed."

"Too small," I said, stroking the bark of my tree, which was the perfect color for the edging I needed. I couldn't believe my luck. "This is the one."

"Uncle Jesse, you don't understand," Lata said, a gentle firmness in her voice. "You can't take that tree. It would endanger the survival of the whole stand, so it wouldn't be sustainable. I checked for you — sent photos to one of the foreman at the Menominee lumberyard. He was surprised to see how well they'd established themselves. He didn't know this variety of yellow birch would grow this far south, and he was kind enough to explain which trees to cut in order to best ensure their survival going into the future. I'm sure you can adapt your design to use narrower boards."

She looked at me with the same stubborn face Charlotte had used every time she talked about the oak — the tree she saved by burning down the house. MY house. A fury buried for more than 40 years rose up like a sudden flame, the heat reddening my face.

"What do you know about my design?" I bellowed with such force that it should have knocked her down. "I'll be damned if I'll let you destroy my life over a tree like you did with the oak. This is my property. I do what I want with it."

Lata's eyes were placid and kind. She put her hand gently on my arm. "Of course, you're upset. I would be too. But it isn't about one tree. That oak is what made possible this whole forest. And this birch ensures the establishment of this species, possibly for the whole region. Adapting your design is a small price to pay for that, don't you think?"

It was eerie, how calm she was, how patient, even as I panted with rage. In the face of it, I felt suddenly embarrassed, as though I were acting like a child. I put my hand on the trunk of the birch. So much at stake. I had to be careful not to alienate her.

"Now that you know the yellow birch are really here," Lata said, "let me show you the rest of the forest."

On we walked, with Lata pointing out this rare native shrub, that rare medicine plant. I can't say I followed what she was saying: my mind was racing all the while, scheming how best to handle this so I could leave with a signed contract — or at least have one by tomorrow. But the longer we walked, the more animated she became with all she was pointing out, and by the time we'd circled around the side of the property and back to the front porch, I understood what she was trying to tell me: Just like the oak, just like the birch, everything on this piece of land was too precious and rare to bulldoze.

"It's remarkable what Aunt Charlotte was able to do here using only library books and her own observations," Lata said. "I know you can appreciate it since you work in sustainability."

I looked at her blankly, groping for words, then said with false brightness, "I'm sure the tech company will be

thrilled to have a park filled with rare native plants along-side their new building."

Lata's face fell. "You don't mean that."

"Mean what? Lata, we're talking almost two million dollars here," I said, exaggerating a little. "That's what the broker is saying, given the excitement around the butterflies — and guaranteed, once they know about the rare plants. You don't have to worry. The buyers are forward thinking. They'll take good care of it."

"By bulldozing the trees for an office building?"

"It'll inspire them to use truly sustainable design. And I'm sure they'll transplant everything that's rare." I patted her arm, playing the part of the older man. "You'll see. They're good people. I promise."

She brushed my hand away. "This is a forest, Uncle Jesse, not a decorative garden for a corporate real estate complex."

"Lata, please. Get real. You're standing on a big city lot. When sold, it converts into an exceptionally comfortable old age — for you and for me. Your mother told me you have no savings. What do you expect to do?"

Lata looked up into the pines. The dappled sunlight formed patterns on her face. "I expect to die, Uncle Jesse—to grow old if I'm lucky, and then to die, while this forest lives on and on."

By THE TIME we had made our way past the jack pines to the path by the sunroom, the mist had turned again to rain. Millie appeared as if out of nowhere and grabbed my hand.

"Let's go inside," she said, pulling me in the direction

of the sunroom.

I hesitated. I hadn't been in that room since before Charlotte died.

The soft weight of Lata's hand rested on my arm. "We could go on the porch, if you'd rather." Her empathy threw me off balance. I shook it off and climbed through the sunroom window.

There was Charlotte's green armchair, the stuffing now coming out, having served as supply for some animal's nest. There was the familiar fireplace with its embossed metal face, empty mouth swept clean, a few candles burning inside, a few others in glass jars scattered around the room. On the floor in front of the fireplace lay a futon covered in an Indian bedspread the color of whiskey, along with a smattering of bed pillows. It formed a nest where Millie now lounged, a pile of books at her elbow. The candles gave the room a welcoming glow, and I had a vague memory of Charlotte in the chair reading by candlelight after she had announced that she was giving up electricity.

"You don't have to stand," Millie said, looking at me. "You can sit with us."

"Unless you prefer the chair?" Lata said as she stepped in over the low windowsill. Behind her fluttered an orange butterfly, dreamlike in the mist. Three of them hung from the eaves of the roof, taking shelter from the rain. I watched as Lata kicked off her shoes and folded herself comfortably into the pillows beside Millie, her face warmed in the light of the candles.

I unlaced my boots, left them under the window and padded over to the pillows. Although I was used to chairs

and found the floor uncomfortable, something about being in the softness with Lata and Millie appealed to me.

Lata poured milky tea from an old thermos into three metal cups, the air now thick with the aroma of fresh ginger. She handed one to each of us just as the rain started to come a little harder, tapping loudly on the metal roof. I could see it beginning to seep through a crack near the ceiling and draw a thin line down the wall. Beneath the line sat a rusted steel pail to catch the drips.

"This tea is the best," Millie said.

Even before I tasted it, I had to agree. Something about the smell of fresh ginger mixing with the fragrance of rain and wet earth that drifted in through the window. I took a sip of tea from the cup — green enamel over steel. I was sure I had used these for camping.

"Where did you unearth these from?" I said to Lata, indicating the cup. "And my old boots? You've been excavating the ruins?"

"They were in a box in the fruit cellar, along with some other things that have come in handy."

"Charlotte must have stored them there," I said. "She used the fruit cellar for her gardening supplies." What else might be down there? I'd have a look when the rain let up.

We sat together in silence, sipping our tea as the candles flickered in the fireplace. Millie slid a large, heavy book out from the bottom of the pile at her elbow and cracked it open. It was some sort of guidebook to native plants, like the ones Charlotte used to keep next to her armchair. The drips of rainwater falling into the pail drummed steadily. It would be easy enough to fix that gap

with a bit of calking.

"How long have you been staying here?" I said to Lata, half imagining Charlotte would answer, tell me she'd never left.

"Just since I arrived from India. The futon was already here. Millie's sister, Calla, left it when she went away to college. She started coming here when she was a child. It inspired her to study sustainable forestry."

"You've ventured a long way from home," I said, taking another sip of tea. "Charlotte never left this yard. Why do you admire her so much?"

"She put her whole self into this piece of land and brought it back from the dead," Lata said. "What's not to admire?"

"Her life was small. And it didn't exactly end on a cheery note."

"That doesn't negate what she left behind. She knew what she valued and did her best with what she had to work with. Who could do more than that?"

I felt a wave of irritation. What about the Victorian house I put so much of myself into? Didn't that count for anything?

"She planted a few things. So what? It's just an over-grown lot," I said, but my words lacked conviction.

Millie slammed her book shut. "It's a forest, Uncle Jesse. Can't you see? A magic forest."

I looked out the window. The wind had picked up and the strong scent of pine wafted in, trees swaying softly in the mist. A warbler chirped from the branch of a white pine and butterflies fluttered under the eaves. There was no

mistaking the magic. I turned and looked at Lata. From this angle, she looked so remarkably like Charlotte that I wondered if she was lying, saying she was Lata. Not impossible — after all, nothing seemed to be as it was supposed to be.

Lata put her hand gently on my leg. "Uncle Jesse, to you this is just a city lot, but growing up in the city, my soul depended on little islands of wildness. It was all I had. It was all Calla had. Now it's all Millie has—and the butterflies. Everyone has a different role to play. They all have value if we do what we do for the right reason."

"And who decides what the right reason might be?"

Millie sighed and rolled her eyes. "Don't be stupid, Uncle Jesse. There's only ever been one right reason and that's love for the earth and everyone who lives here. Didn't your mother teach you anything?"

Lata smiled. I couldn't help but smile, too.

"You look cold," Lata said to me. "That sweater you're wearing is kind of thin."

I hadn't noticed, but she was right. I was shivering.

Lata reached under a pillow next to Millie and pulled out a folded wool blanket. She shook it open and wrapped it around my shoulders. I recognized it immediately. It was the blanket Charlotte had brought to the truck when we first met at the construction site all those years ago. It felt heavy and warm, like a cocoon, and smelled of musty lavender.

I took another sip of tea. The rain fell soft on the metal roof. Outside the window, a hummingbird hovered for a moment, then darted into the pines. The warmth of the blanket, dimness of the room, flickering candles — I started to feel drowsy. I put my tea aside and lay back into the pillows. Drops of rain falling into the steel pail drummed like a heartbeat.

A feeling came over me that just for now I wouldn't fight. After all those years of being alone in the world, restless and unmoored, it was the unfamiliar feeling of coming home.

THE END

OR IS IT THE BEGINNING?

Afterword

MORE THAN 25 YEARS AGO, I found myself haunted by the image of a woman standing in the attic window of a burning house, waving. This book was born from that image, its narrative and characters morphing, stretching and contracting over the years to hold the deep explorations I was making into ancestral trauma, disturbing environmental trends, and the difficulties I had navigating a culture increasingly focused on a competitive marketplace mentality at the expense of soulful living and intimate connection to the natural world and to one another.

This book is an artifact from that process. It helped me to write it, as it gave a narrative structure to what otherwise were free-floating images and concerns that had no home. While it is as personal and quirky in its symbolism as a dream, like a dream it also holds archetypal elements that might speak to others and serve them in some way, even if just as encouragement to write their own story. I share it for this reason.

OVER THE COURSE OF THESE YEARS, many people have contributed to the explorations that went into this story. First, there was my Grandma Brewer, whose early encouragement to keep my heart and mind open to the invisible made possible numinous experiences that otherwise are stamped out early in a materialist culture.

She was born and raised on the Menominee Reservation, something she never spoke of and that I didn't know until after she died. Like many Native American children, she was taken from her family at a young age (only 10) and put into a government boarding school that was run by the Catholic Church. The trauma and internalized racism instilled in the children at that school tore her family apart, and I still feel the reverberations of this trauma today, in myself and in the culture at large.

Even with this trauma in her life, my grandmother didn't lose her gentleness, her connection to spirit and her open-heartedness. I was haunted by all that had happened to her immediate family and tribe, and it spurred me to learn all I could about the tragic injustices that the government has perpetrated against the Menominee and that indigenous people all over the world have endured.

THE LATE GEORGE AND LOUISE SPINDLER, anthropologists who lived among the Menominee in the 50s and did extensive interviews with elders and other tribal members, were of great help to me early in my exploration. I read their book, *Dreamers with Power,* and subsequently spent time with them at their home in Calistoga, California, and at their cabin at Moose Lake in Wisconsin on the edge of the reservation. They were generous and loving as they formed the first bridge for me to begin piecing together what had been lost in my grandmother's generation.

MY MOTHER'S COUSIN, FATHER BERNARD BRUNETTE, a priest who grew up near the reservation, took me on two driving tours there — to the family house, the cemeteries where various relatives were buried, and the mission church my great grandmother Jane Brunette had cared for, where between Catholic masses when the priest was away, outlawed Menominee ceremonies were held. He introduced me to Sister Regis, a cousin of his, then in her 90s, and both told me stories of the family and passed on all they knew. After he died, he left me a beautiful hand-beaded necklace with the insignia of three thunderbirds which had been gifted to him in the 70s by a relative after he presided over my Great Aunt Mary's funeral on the reservation.

SERENDIPITY AND LUCK allowed me to learn of an innovative five-day seminar being held at the Menominee reservation in 2005 to train Wisconsin teachers in tribal history. I asked permission to attend, though I was not a Wisconsin teacher, and flew from California to spend those five days in a powerful and deep learning. The generosity of the tribal elders was astounding to me, and I learned far more than historical information as they welcomed us into their hearts and their forest home.

What I learned that week created the foundation for a growing awareness and healing for myself and my ancestors that continues to this day. Such deep gratitude particularly to Menominee elders Audrey and Wabeno, as well as Lisa Poupart and Margaret Snow, who taught me many things, such as the dedication, strength and resilience of those who stayed on the reservation and preserved the culture and stories as best they could, the power of the talking circle as it is practiced traditionally, as well as the power of praying with tobacco as offering and holder of intention, and of tying our prayers to the natural world.

Gratitude again to Lisa Poupart for inviting me to audit my first ever online class in 2005 on Wisconsin Native American History. I learned a great deal that shook my world and opened my eyes to the things that had never been spoken of or taught in our school system. It is people like Lisa who work hard to rectify that.

IN AUGUST OF 2017, My sister Mary, her husband Terry and I brought my 90-year-old mother to the reservation for the first pow wow she had ever attended. She was so moved by the beautiful dancing in the forest amphitheatre and the hospitality of the tribe. She had come a long way from the days when she would say again and again, "your Aunt Mary is an Indian," but never that my grandmother was Menominee and so all of us shared this heritage.

Such is the power of intergenerational trauma — my grandmother's need to hide her identity to survive the cruel racism in the government boarding school and the culture at large, subliminally passing on that fear to her children. All those years later at the pow wow, my mother was able to fully embrace this heritage, smiling and laughing and enjoying the beauty of it all. I am so happy this could happen that summer, for she died a year later.

IN 2014, I LEARNED ABOUT THE DAYAK BENUAQ PEOPLE of Muara Tae, Borneo, whose rainforest home was being illegally destroyed for palm oil plantations. I visited their forest on two occasions. It was the pain of my own ancestral loss of forest and tribe that drove me there, and I was grateful for all I learned about their struggle to preserve their forest and lifeways from the powerful forces that came to bulldoze and destroy — just as had happened to my grandmother's tribe. Much learning came through the collaboration between myself, activist Ambrosius (Ruwi) Ruwindrijarto, Pak Asuy and other tribal elders to raise the funds for a large-scale shamanic ceremony to protect their rainforest and heal the rifts in their tribe. We wouldn't have raised the $16,000 without Tesa Silvestre, who with great heart and enthusiasm, used her bountiful skills to gather an international circle of friends to help with the crowd-funding campaign — perhaps the first in history to have the creation of 10 ceremonial spears for the shamans as one of the budget lines.

MORE GRATITUDE TO THE SHAPIBO HEALERS, Maestro Damian and Maestra Lila, whose ceremonies in the Amazon jungle in 2016 helped to firmly reconnect me to the ancestors and wider web of life that had been disturbed by the trauma in my Grandmother's generation. I was especially moved when at the second ceremony, I shyly wore the thunderbird necklace passed down to me from Father Bernard, and Lila laughed and pointed and smiled. She told the translator to tell me we were from the same lineage — that her spiritual name meant "Thunderbird."

AS FOR THE WRITING OF THE STORY ITSELF, gratitude to writers more masterful than me whose stories served as inspiration and scaffolding for places I got stuck, especially Marilyn Robinson's *Housekeeping,* Michael Cunningham's *Speciman Days,* Jean Rhys' *Wide Sargasso Sea,* and Louise Erdrich's *Love Medicine.*

A big thanks to Judy Woodburn, whose sensitive reading of my initial short story on this topic gave me the confidence to keep pursuing it further as it took me on this journey into history and family. To finally give her a copy of the finished book will truly be coming full circle.

Thanks also to Sarah Stone and Andy Couturier, who encouraged me to keep going when it was getting particularly difficult to navigate the layers that were calling for expression, and to my big sister Chris Hanselman, who let me know how deeply she "got it" just at a time when I most needed to hear it.

Thanks to my Facebook friends who cheered me on and offered to read earlier drafts as I muddled through the many attempts to end this story in a way that was honest, life-affirming and somehow satisfying to my psyche. Getting the input of such a wide cross-section of people, rather than just from a few writers in a workshop setting, proved invaluable for me to understand who and what the story was really for.

I want to especially thank Siri Barker, Richard Bock, Mark Brewer, Tom Butts, Mary Kay Cahill, Carol Degnan Deleskiewicz, Mary Degnan Mrowiec, Ken Farber, Suzi Garner, Louisa Gluck, Kevin Heal, Joanna Intara Zim, Meriam Marie Jose, Phyllis Matyi, Dan Middleton, Julie Neumann, Linda Kay Stevens, Sonja Valez and Suki Zöe for their careful reading and comments. Your feedback and support was deeply appreciated. If I missed anyone, please forgive me. It's been a long process.

DEEP GRATITUDE TO FRANK ECHENHOFER, who read the story aloud with me and took it in with such depth that I was able to see my way to an ending that felt real and true — something I had been struggling with for years before his deep listening gave me the mirror I needed to be clear on what I most wanted to say.

Perhaps this ending is not completely satisfying to the reader, as in some ways things are too tied up and in other ways, too incomplete, but I finally realized that the story can't be written to satisfy only my literary aesthetics, since the whole point is to shine a light on the spiral of lineage that winds through the generations. Given this, the true end of this story is not one that I can write alone — it is something that all of us have to write together as we choose to support life, love and soul, generation after generation.

FOR ME, THIS STORY IS NOT JUST PERSONAL, it is also collective. Yes, it is about the effort to preserve two small forests on large city lots. But to preserve a small stand of trees is to preserve the forests of the world. I learned from Asuy, a knowledge holder of the Dayak Benuaq, of the importance of these little islands of wildness. When Asuy was giving me and Ruwi a tour of the destroyed part of their forest, there was a tiny island of trees in the center of a field of palm oil. I pointed to it and said sadly that they might as well take that out. Asuy shook his head and said this tiny island of trees was precious. One day, people would no longer care about the palm oil. Something would be found to replace it and these fields would be abandoned. Then, his people would come back to restore what they could of the forest.

That tiny island of trees would shelter the plants that they would put around it, allowing them to eventually meet with the plantings on either side — just as Lata described in the first chapter of this story, when she spoke of the islands of wildness along the edge of the cemetery.

Asuy made it clear to me that to preserve the forest is not a grand gesture or something that can be done in one generation by a few activists. In the larger scheme of things, it means a great deal to save a tiny stand of trees when the forests are in danger. There is no act too small to make a real difference. Each of us can do our best with what we have to sustain life, love and soul in our corner of the world. Together, we create these islands of hope, making it possible for us to stitch together the places where the soul of the world has been torn apart.

THANK YOU FOR READING this deeply felt, deeply personal story of my soul. If you ever decide to write your own, please share it with me and with others who might be touched. I would be so honored to join with you in the depths of what you care about.

— *Jane Brunette*
Sacred Valley, Peru, June 2019

About the author

JANE BRUNETTE teaches and writes about meditation, spirituality and creating a soulful life in challenging times. She created Writing from the Soul, an approach to writing that has sprouted groups around the world, and she mentors individuals in writing and spiritual practice.

Trained as a psychotherapist and authorized as a Dharma teacher, she has traveled widely, living simply in cultures where this is still possible to free her time and her mind for meditation, spiritual practice and retreat.

In addition to *Lineage of the Trees*, she is the author of two collections of poetry, *Cartoon Kali* and *Grasshopper Guru,* as well as *The Big and the Small: A Soul Story.* Her websites are writingfromthesoul.net and flamingseed.com.

Printed in Great Britain
by Amazon